Acknowledgement

BWL Publishing Inc. recognizes the Cultural Industry Book Publishers Operating Grant from the Province of Alberta for the funding allocation and support provided to BWL Publishing Inc.

Alberta
Government

Ravens on the Red Road
Phil L'Hirondelle and
John Wisdomkeeper

Print ISBNs
Amazon Print 9780228628170
Indigo Spark 9780228628187
Barnes & Noble 9780228630609
BWL Print 9780228628194

http://bwlpublishing.ca

Table of Contents

Prologue

His fingers tightened against the flesh of her throat, stifling her screams and forcing her eyes to bulge in terror.

His free hand played along the neckline of her cotton blouse, his groin pulsed and his breath came in short juddering gasps as he savored his power.

He gathered her blouse into a tight ball, twisting and rending the flimsy threads that barely covered her nakedness. The fabric tore and gave way, and his eyes feasted on heavy brown breasts. Trembling, he pressed his palm against her nipples, parted his lips and rolled his tongue over his teeth.

She struggled beneath his grasp, and he tightened his grip squeezing until her movements stopped. Excitement stirred him. He moved his hand along her plump legs and slid between her thighs. A low cry rose in his throat. Blood roared through his veins and he sank his teeth into her breast. The sweet red liquid spurted against his lips and crazed him. Crying out his release, he tightened his fingers into her throat and wrenched her neck back and forth until a vertebrae snapped.

Her grotesque death mask mocked him. He reached for a pillow and covered her face, but the pristine white case made a nothing of what he'd done, and the salt of her blood stung his lips.

He started to shake and fear struck like a cobra.

"I've got to get her out of here," he whimpered, then froze at the sound of footsteps. He'd thought all the students had left. Who could that be out there. On silent feet, he crept to the door. His fingers groped for the deadbolt and found it fastened. He waited. The footsteps faded and he heard the sound of the outside door closing.

Someone must have forgotten something. They're gone now, but I've got to get her out of here. Fear like bile rose in his throat and he choked it back down. He stayed crouched, waiting until his legs ached and his arms twitched. Silence reigned. There were no more footsteps. Opening the door and slipping outside he reached the garage, started the big Mercedes and pulled it around back of the building. There he opened the trunk, checked again to make sure no one was around, then he raced inside, grabbed the blanket wrapped body and dumped it into the trunk. Making sure he had his bag, he locked the doors behind him, got into the driver's seat of the German sedan, and drove off into the night.

It was pitch dark when he entered the Park. Past closing time, but he had a buzzer that allowed him to open the gates. Driving to his pre-selected spot, he steered the car into what was little more than a brush covered trail and inched along until he was sure he wouldn't be seen in the unlikely event someone else was loitering in the park after closing.

Opening the trunk, he lifted his burden and carried it to the clearing. There he laid her out inside the circle of stones he'd made earlier.

"Now, my dear, you'll be famous." He giggled and then switched to a kind of high pitched keening, as he removed her clothes and spread her so he had her arms stretched out one on either side and her legs spread apart to leave her genitals exposed.

"They'll love this," he cackled, as he held up a pale blue card then turned it around to show a picture of a rattlesnake curled around a nest of eggs. Taking an ordinary kitchen knife out of his bag, he pushed it through the top of the card, and then gripping the knife by the handle he stabbed it into the fleshy part of her breast.

"Now you're a beautiful maiden that some Indian's sacrificed to one of his Gods. Oh yes, the police are going to have a lovely time rousting all those Indians while they try and find which one did you this way."

Stepping back from his grisly stage, he picked up his bag and blanket and slipped back out of the woods, recovered the big black car, and drove out of the Park.

Chapter One

"You ready to go?" Dez Pallaton poked his head around the door of Martine LaChance's office and gave her a friendly smile. He had his long black hair pulled into a ponytail and a colorful scarf tied around his forehead.

"Wow, don't you look dashing!" Martine looked up from her desk to let her eyes drink in the more than six feet of man grinning at her like a boy with a secret. "What's the occasion?"

"Don't tell me you've forgotten the circle Wisdomkeeper and Phil are holding over at the Remand Centre?"

"Damn." Martine clapped her hands to her face, then peeked out through her fingers at Dez's dismayed expression and laughed.

"Of course I haven't forgotten." She grinned at him and reached into her desk drawer for her shoulder bag. "I'm meeting Marcia and Diane at Pacific Centre. We're planning an extended tour of Robson Street followed by a long leisurely lunch at Joeys." She picked up her cell phone, tossed it in the bag and walked over to Dez. Tall and leggy with jet black hair that hung to her waist,

Martine turned heads everywhere she went, but she and Dez had something really good going and neither one of them paid any attention to the yearning looks they attracted when they appeared together as a couple.

Both of them worked out of the Vancouver Friendship Centre, Dez as a police liaison for Indigenous street youth and Martine as a family response worker. They loved their jobs, so when they made the decision to come out as a couple, they'd also made it clear that their personal life would never interfere with their work. For the past two years they'd stuck to that and everyone they worked with knew them as a hard working couple and had no issues with their personal relationship.

Even though they considered themselves a couple, they each had their own condo, side by side in the same building. It worked for them, and Martine especially valued having her own space. Lately Dez had been thinking a lot about making things a lot more consolidated. He even had an ostentatiously large and criminally expensive diamond ring stashed in a velvet lined case with his private collection, and if all went well, he was planning on asking the big question the end of August when the Blue Moon was due to make an appearance. He still wasn't sure what Martine's reaction was going to be, but he planned on giving it a try, and if she said no, he'd just keep the ring on standby for when she eventually would come to her senses.

* * *

Dez and Martine let Annie, the Friendship Centre's receptionist, know they'd be gone for the day, and both of them climbed into Dez's Jeep Cherokee.

"Before we get started," Martine turned towards Dez, leaned in and molded her lips to his. "Mmm!" He returned the kiss with matching ardor, letting his tongue part her lips and entwine in a passionate dance.

"Okay." Martine pulled back. "We either quit that or we head home and you miss your Circle."

Dez sighed. "Don't tempt me."

"It's taken you six months to get this set up, so I know darn well you're not serious. Let's go, so you have time to drop me off before you're due to meet up with Phil and Wisdomkeeper."

After dropping Martine, Dez headed for the Remand Centre. Parking at Hastings and Main was no picnic, and it took the better part of 20 minutes to finally snag a spot on the street left by a departing pickup.

Great. Phil said to meet out front so we could all go in together. Let's hope everyone's on time.

Dez needn't have worried. As he rounded the corner of the grey cement building, he spotted Phil and Wisdomkeeper leaning against the wall beside the front entrance.

"Welcome, brother." Phil gripped Dez's outstretched hand. "You remember John Wisdomkeeper."

"I do. Good to see you," Dez shook hands with the tall dark-haired man who welcomed him with a smile.

"We'd best get inside then," Phil picked up his pipe case and the two men followed him through the door to where a female guard beckoned for them to stop.

"You can't bring that case inside," she told Phil.

"We're actually here to conduct a pipe ceremony for the inmates." Phil explained. "This bag contains my sacred pipe and it's necessary for the ceremony."

No sooner had Phil said his piece about the pipe than the electric doors leading into the main lobby as well as those leading out to the courtyard where the ceremony would be held slid open.

"The power of the pipe." Wisdomkeeper said and Phil nodded agreement.

Dez smiled and followed the other two out into the courtyard.

* * *

The remand center was four city blocks square and four stories high. A razor wire topped box, 4x4x4 with armed guards

14

carrying M4 rifles and patrolling the gun walk.

We entered the courtyard and both of us thanked the Creator for the open sky. It was more than we'd hoped for and was a good sign.

There were about 100 men in the courtyard. Most didn't know much about our Indigenous old ways, but a handful knew some of the songs and a smaller handful spoke their native tongue.

There were only a few inmates from BC, but in the general population half the inmates were Indigenous, with many from the Prairies and Ontario. They were mostly Cree and Ojibway. Four of them in particular stood out. They hung together in their small group, separated from the rest of the inmates, and both Wisdomkeeper and Phil felt something off about them. The older one, who seemed to be their leader, was white while two of the others were Metis and one of them appeared to be a full blood indigenous, probably Cree.

The white guy smirked through most of the ceremonies and the other three followed his lead. All of them acted like their time was being wasted. That wasn't the issue though; both Phil and Wisdomkeeper were used to non-believers and even hecklers, but the reactions from these guys spooked both of them. Every time they looked at any of the four, but especially the leader, there was a tangible and negative change in the latent charge in the air between the men. It was spooky the way the hair on both men's arms stood up and their skin burned whenever they looked at any of the men in that group.

Phil figured they'd need some help with this gathering, so he asked the Creator to give them a show of support. Boy, did he get an answer to that one. They started the ceremony, and Phil advised, "Keep an eye on the sky when we take out our pipes".

He and Wisdomkeeper lifted their pipes together pointing the stems toward Father Sky, and hardly were the words out of Phil's mouth when a huge bolt of lightning flashed across the sky accompanied by a boom so loud it shook the prison. Awed looks, and even some confused were visible on the faces of everyone on the yard.

Everyone's attention had been captured, and afterwards, everyone, including the three Native guys in the hostile-acting gang, listened to every word Phil and Wisdomkeeper shared for the rest of the Ceremony.

"If we could get one or two of those guys away from the white dude I think we might get through to them," Wisdomkeeper said, and Phil nodded agreement.

"I'll go get whitey's attention and maybe you can focus on the youngest one of that group. He's Metis, and from the way he hung onto our words in the ceremonies, I'd say he's already having second thoughts about their self-appointed leader."

Phil and Wisdomkeeper moved into the crowd, stopping here and there to answer questions and talk with the men. Phil reached his destination first, and as if acknowledging the other's position, he spoke directly to the leader.

"I didn't get your name," Phil said, "I hope you got something personally out of today's ceremonies."

"Calvin. That was some trick you pulled with the thunder and lightnin. Guess you've got a contact with the weather guys?"

Phil smiled, knowing it was never worth arguing a point with guys like that. "So how long will you figure to be inside?" he asked.

"As short as I can make it." Calvin's smug smile got those hairs standing up and his arms stinging again. "Good to hear," Phil said. "Nothing like good behavior to shorten up a sentence. Good talking to you," Phil noted that Wisdomkeeper had finished with the young guy and he made his excuses, leaving the creepy Calvin to mix with the thinning crowd.

* * *

"That guy's Bad Medicine. If I was the warden of this place, I'd be watching those four", Phil said as he met up with Wisdomkeeper. After stowing their pipes back in Phil's case, the two of them headed towards where Dez was waiting at the exit.

"What did you think?" Phil asked Dez.

"It was great. More than I expected. How in heck did you arrange that lightning strike?" Dez gave Phil a quizzical look.

"Just good timing, I guess." Phil said with a wink, and Wisdomkeeper nodded agreement.

"Okay. Guess I can't argue. Just glad to be on your good sides." The three men walked through the opening doors and past the checkout.

"Thanks again," Dez said. "You really made today special for a lot of guys."

"All My Relations" Phil said, acknowledging the thanks.

"I touched base with one of the young guys," Wisdomkeeper said. "He's part of that tough looking group hanging around in there, but I've a gut feeling if we can get him away from that white dude he's hanging with he could be salvageable. Anyway, I'd like to give it a try if he reaches out. I gave him my card and he said he'd be in touch when he got released. We'll see what happens."

Phil nodded agreement and they took leave of Dez, walking to their truck along a doorless side of the remand on an industrial side street devoid of other pedestrians.

Chapter Two

Back at the office Dez went to work on a funding proposal that he had to have submitted by end of day. In the middle of a calculation, his phone buzzed, and he touched the speaker button. "Yeah," he grumbled.

"We've got one of yours." The voice of Detective Mark Hanson growled through the receiver. "She's been strangled."

"What makes you think she's mine?"

"She's about fifteen, looks streetwise—she's Native. How soon can you get down here?"

"Give me twenty minutes." Dez set the receiver in its cradle and stared, unseeing, at the funding proposal on his desk. Had somebody killed one of his kids? His cop friends were always preaching detachment. How in hell was he supposed to do that? Dez understood these kids. His mom was Ojibway and he considered himself Native, even though his dad was one of those Irish, Indian, French mixtures that Canadians referred to as Métis. The Native kids trusted Dez, which was a lot more than they did most white men.

"I need a coffee." Dez left his desk and headed for the lunchroom. Annie was inside taking her morning break. She greeted him with a wave.

"How's it going?" Dez noted the bulge in Annie's cheek and the half-eaten donut in her hand.

She flashed her eyes at him and he laughed. Even though Dez kept his black hair neatly braided, and dressed office casual, his good looks and toned body drew a lot of sultry looks from female coworkers, but Dez was definitely a one-woman man, and that woman was more than a double handful.

Taking the coffee back to his desk Dez picked up his pencil and focused on the proposal. Twenty minutes later, he stopped at Annie's desk with an envelope. "Dim Sum's on me if you'll get this typed and on the Director's desk by three o'clock."

Annie giggled. "I'll hold you to that," she told his retreating back.

* * *

Vancouver police headquarters covered two full blocks and finding a parking space took fortitude. Dez circled, made a sharp turn onto Cordova and hit the brakes. An old wino stepped in front of the Jeep and flipped him the bird.

Dez shook his head and laughed. Yesterday was Welfare Wednesday. The old boozer would be back in the soup line tomorrow, but today he had a bottle of cheap wine clutched in his hand and change jingling in his pocket. He was King for a day.

A VW Beetle pulled away from the curb and Dez angled the Cherokee for approach. It took some doing to snug a Jeep into a spot left by a Bug, but he'd had plenty of practice. Safely squeezed into the space, he locked the doors and crossed the street.

Inside the double doors, Dez stopped at the front desk. "I'm going up to see Hanson."

The desk clerk looked up from a magazine, nodded his head and went back to reading.

As usual, Dez bypassed the elevator and took the steps to the third floor. At the end of the hall, he stopped in front of a corner office, knocked once, and stepped inside.

"Good, you're here." Detective Hanson motioned to the wooden chair fronting his desk. "You remember Carver?" The detective indicated the tall, dark-skinned native who stood with his shoulder propped against the window frame.

"Sure. How's it going, Frank?"

Carver nodded in return.

"Well, now that you're here." Hanson hoisted his 240-pound frame out of the chair, pulled open a file drawer and removed a glossy black and white. "See if you recognize this girl." He handed over the photo and Dez found himself looking at a bruised and bloated face inset with sightless dead eyes.

His stomach clenched. "She doesn't look familiar but it's hard to tell from this. Where'd they find her?"

"One of the guards checking out the west-end of the Park where the bums bed down stumbled across her body. Doc says she was killed somewhere else and dumped."

"Raped?"

Hanson nodded. "We figure an Indian killed her."

"How's that?"

"They found her stripped and staked out like she was an offering in a ritual. Her arms and legs had been tied with buckskin and she had this card stuck to her breast."

Hanson held up a pale blue card. "Carver says it's a Medicine Card." He turned the card to reveal a picture of a rattlesnake curled around a nest of eggs.

"That's a Medicine Card, all right." Dez took the card out of Hanson's hand. "That still doesn't explain why you think the killer is Native. You can buy these cards at every New Age shop in the city. Besides, Natives are superstitious and messing with the Medicine Cards is taboo."

"Well, killing people's also taboo and this bastard didn't mind that."

Hanson reached out his hand for the card and Dez held it back. "You said the card was stuck on her. How?"

"With this." Hanson reached into the envelope and pulled out a kitchen knife. "Carver says these Medicine Cards mean something. You know anything about them?”

“No, but I know someone who does. Let me take him the card and see what he says.”

“Are you nuts? This is evidence. If the Sergeant found out I let you take a card out of evidence he’d have me back on the street handing out parking tickets.”

“Easy money.” Dez chuckled at the vision of Hanson’s belly stuffed inside a uniform. Then he cut the grin. “Seriously Mark, I’d like Wisdomkeeper to look at this. He’s an elder I know and he reads the Medicine Cards.”

Hanson scowled. “Bring him in then.”

Dez shook his head. “Wisdomkeeper’s one of the old timers. His memory goes back to the days when white cops beat the shit out of Indians for entertainment. I can’t say he’s never been inside a police station, but it wasn’t ever his idea.”

“Damn fools.” Hanson shook his head.

Dez, not knowing whether Hanson meant Wisdomkeeper or the white cops, kept silent.

Finally, Hanson grunted out of his chair and walked over to the photocopy machine. “I’ll make a copy for you. Take it along to the old man and see what he says. I’ll expect a report.”

“Thanks. I’m going to take a run out there this weekend. I’ll let you know if he has any ideas.”

Once outside of headquarters Dez retrieved the Jeep, stopped by the Friendship Center to make sure Annie had turned in his proposal, reiterated his promise to take her for Dim Sum, and headed home.

The details of the girl's murder had Dez worried. It took a lot of juggling to maintain harmony in a large multicultural city like Vancouver. The way the press would play this up if they got any hint of a ritual murder could spark the kind of racial tension that would make his job even tougher than it already was. The Native community remembered all too vividly the routs of the 1950's when the Canadian government—hellbent on reforming savages—gave their Indian agents instructions to round-up Native kids, take them away from their families, and force them into residential schools. The divide between Indian and White ran deep. Most Natives would read about the murder in the media and immediately jump to the conclusion that yet another Native brother was being set up to pay for a white man's crime.

Dez eased along Commercial Drive to Adanac and turned into the alley behind an attractive two-story colonial. The square frame and brick structure housed a Chinese grocery on the ground floor and a pair of condos on top. Dez had purchased the property before the latest boom had sent Vancouver's housing skyrocketing. The double garage attached to the property had sold him on the place. It was a decision he'd never regretted.

Dez used to live in one of the condos and keep the other vacant. That had changed when the Friendship Center hired a young Métis woman from Quebec. Director Sandstone, mindful of Vancouver's housing crisis, pleaded with Dez to rent his second condo to their new associate. Dez resisted at first, unwilling to relinquish his privacy, but then he'd met Martine.

Silky black hair hung long and straight to her waist and Dez's eyes followed miles of leg from the hem of her mini-skirt to the strappy leather sandals on her feet.

"Dez. This is our new associate Martine LaChance." The Director had said, "I've told her you might be able to help with finding accommodations." Director Sandstone had brought Martine into Dez's office and stood there with a self-satisfied smile on her lips when Dez's face took on the startled gaze of a deer caught in headlights.

"Hi." Martine fixed her melting chocolate eyes on Dez's coal black orbs. Stunned by the fire in his belly and the tangle of his tongue, Dez stuttered through introductions and arranged a showing of his condo. Remembering those early days had Dez squirming. He'd taken Martine through the condo and they'd gone to his place to work out the details. Dez gave her the lease and while she read it over, he admired her obvious assets. When Martine finished reading, she signed her name, and handed the lease back to Dez. Then she let out a long-suffering sigh. "Just so there's no misunderstanding," she'd said. "I'm flattered by your obvious interest, but I never get personally involved with my co-workers." The look on her face and the flash in her eyes left no doubt that she'd observed his scrutiny.

That had been two years ago, and the relationship between Dez and Martine had long since progressed to a very satisfying mutual understanding. He kept his condo and she kept hers, and they moved freely back and forth.

Once they'd established the ground rules and found out how much they both enjoyed each other and their living arrangements, they'd come out at work and admitted they were a couple and they'd kept their word that it wouldn't become an issue at the office.

* * *

Dez's living room décor reflected his cultural heritage and his passion for traditional oddities like the scalp collection. Against the wall stood a six-foot oak cabinet with heavy doors and stained-glass inserts. Inside a beat-up leather case lined with faded blue velvet cloth lay Dez's most cherished possession. Wrapped in a swatch of rabbit's fur lay the sacred pipe that he had carved back when he'd been sweating drugs and alcohol out of his system.

Taking the pipe out of its case and strolling out to the patio, Dez settled into a chair and put flame to the small bowl of tobacco. He needed to offer prayers for the young girl's spirit and remind the Creator that getting respect had been a hard struggle for his people. Vancouver was a major improvement over the small Ontario town where Dez and his sister grew up, but the line between white man and Indian never quite went away. Having a brother accused of a ritual sex crime would be a major setback.

After making his offering and saying his prayers, Dez packed the pipe back in its case and stood up to lean against the railing.

Down below, an ethnic mix of Caucasians, Natives, Asians, East Indians and Africans strolled past the pasta houses, delis, coffee shops and fruit stands lining Commercial Drive. Hands of every shape and size picked through boxes of plump red tomatoes, measured sacks of onions, and pinched the flesh of red, yellow, and green peppers. Pungent strings of garlic hung from wooden rafters and fresh cut flowers poked their heads out of baskets and tubs lining the sidewalks.

Dez's patio door slid open and the spicy scent of Opium perfume floated to him on a current of air. He turned his head to meet a pair of eyes the color of rich dark chocolate.

"What's wrong?" Martine touched his arm.

Dez shook his head. "Hanson called this afternoon, they found a dead girl in Stanley Park and he thought she might be one of mine. I didn't recognize her."

Martine's face turned white. "I hope it isn't Shannon." Instinctively she reached for Dez's hand.

"Who's Shannon?"

"One of the girls from my circle. She didn't show up Monday night and I called her brother Alex. He hadn't seen her since the weekend, and the house mother at Evergreen House hasn't seen her since Monday afternoon."

"Maybe she went home?" Most of the girls in Martine's circle came from the reservation, and it wasn't uncommon for one of them to quit the city without telling anyone they were leaving.

She shook her head. "Shannon and Alex are alone in the world. They were in foster care on Vancouver Island. When Alex won a track scholarship to the University of British Columbia he moved over here. Within a month Shannon followed him. He lives in a dorm, so he brought Shannon to the Friendship Centre and we set her up at Evergreen House." Martine turned back and crossed to the patio door. "I'm going to phone and see if he's heard anything."

While Dez waited for Martine's return, he watched an old geezer in a sweat-stained cowboy hat who had stopped in front of the liquor store. The musician lifted a guitar out of a battered case and propped it open- an invitation to passing shoppers to salute his tunes with their coins. Then the old timer swung the worn leather guitar strap over his shoulder and started strumming the opening bars to Roger Miller's King of the Road.

Dez leaned on the railing and listened while keeping an ear out for Martine. It sure seemed to be taking her a long time. Damn, I hope the girl has been found. However, it appeared there'd be no such luck when minutes later Martine stepped through the doorway and the look on her face gave him the bad news.

"Alex still hasn't heard from Shannon." That hushed little girl voice had Dez gripping the rail. "Alex is worried sick. I didn't tell him about the dead girl, but I'd like to see her."

"She's in the morgue. Are you sure?"

"I've got to, for Alex's sake."

"I'll call Mark and clear it with him. Why don't we go to the kitchen? As soon as I've made my call I'll fix some coffee."

"I'll fix the coffee." Martine smiled through moist eyes.

"Deal."

In the kitchen Dez left Martine to mechanically go through the motions of brewing the coffee while he went the bedroom to make his call. He pulled a cell phone out of his pocket and sprawled across his king-sized bed.

"Homicide." Mark Hanson's gruff bark answered Dez's call.

"I might have an ID on the dead girl." Dez said. "Is it possible for us to see her?"

"Sure. I talked to Sam a little while ago. He's finished the autopsy. I'll let him know you're coming. Are you bringing someone to make the ID?"

"Martine. She thinks it's one of the girls from her Monday night circle."

"Better warn her it won't be pleasant."

"I did. She knows. Will you set it up with Sam and give me a call when he's ready?"

"Sure. Might take a while, but I'll get back to you quick as I can."

In the kitchen Dez took the cup of coffee Martine handed over and swung his leg over one of the bar stools.

"Hanson will give us a call as soon as he's arranged for you to see the body."

* * *

"So tell me how did your event at the Remand Center turn out?"

"It was amazing. Phil and Wisdomkeeper are something to watch. I swear they have a first class pass right to the spirit world. You should have seen it. Phil called for a demonstration from the sky when he took out his pipe, and seconds later a streak of lighting flashed and a thunderbolt fairly shook the whole prison. Scared the shit

30

out of the inmates gathered in the courtyard."

"Oh no." Martine clapped her hand to her mouth. "I would love to have seen that."

"Yeah, well you can bet Phil and Wisdomkeeper had their full attention for all the rest of their presentation."

* * *

Dez's cell buzzed and he listened to the response and then put the phone back in his pocket. "We're good to go if you still want to," he said.

"I'll just grab a jacket." Martine stiffened her spine and prepared to face whatever lay ahead.

* * *

Twenty minutes later Dez pulled into the parking garage at Vancouver General Hospital, secured a ticket and located a spot near the Morgue. Once he parked the Jeep he got out, walked around and opened the door for Martine.

"Are you sure you want to do this?" He took her hand and helped her to the ground.

"I'm okay." She leaned briefly into his supporting arms. "I feel kind of sick. I'm sure it's nerves."

"I'll be right here with you." Dez took her hand and they walked around to the side entrance.

"I'm Dez Pallaton, from Street Scene. The coroner's expecting us," Dez said to the young orderly manning the reception desk.

The Morgue, located in the basement of the hospital, could be reached by a flight of steep metal steps, but with Martine along Dez opted for the slightly claustrophobic elevator. In the basement, they walked along a corridor until they came to an office labeled 'Coroner'.

Dez knocked softly and stepped inside. "How's it going, Sam?" He greeted the coroner. "I haven't seen you since Mark's last poker game. How's that boy of yours?"

"Good to see you, Dez." Sam stood and stuck out his hand. "Sam Jr's growing like a weed. He'll be starting school this fall."

"Seems like only yesterday, you were trying to figure out how to change a diaper." Dez grinned at Sam. "This is Martine," he said, indicating the woman beside him. "I guess Hanson called you?"

Sam nodded, then grabbed a ring of keys from a drawer, and stepped around his desk. "It's just down the hall." He led them along a narrow corridor and up to a shiny metal door. "It's cold inside," he warned, as he pulled the handle.

A blast of frigid air met them with the opening of the door, and Dez put a protective arm around Martine's shoulders. The smells of formaldehyde, disinfectant, and something else were omnipresent in the cold storage room.

"Whenever you're ready?" Sam walked over and stood in front of a bank of shiny metal cabinets.

Dez nodded, and Sam pulled out the bottom drawer. "Okay," he said, and lifted the sheet.

Martine gasped and turned her face into Dez's chest.

"You recognize her?" Sam asked

"Yes, it's Shannon," Martine whispered.

"Let's go back to Sam's office." Dez led her back to Sam's office and helped her into his chair. "You sit here for a minute."

"I don't know how I'm going to tell Alex," Martine sobbed. "Shannon was the only family he had. He's going to be devastated."

"The police are trained to handle this kind of thing, if you'd rather not do it yourself."

"No! I want to tell him. Alex asked me to look out for Shannon, and I placed her in Evergreen House. They don't have any family, and I feel responsible." She brushed at her eyes. "Will you come with me?"

"Of course. I'll call Hanson and let him know, then we can head over there."

"Can you take me home first? I need a little time before I face Alex."

"Sure. I'll tell Sam we're going."

* * *

Dez left Martine at the door to her condo. Inside his living room, he settled into the recliner and grabbed the phone.

"We've just come from the morgue," he said, when Mark answered his ring. "Martine identified the dead girl."

"Let me grab a pad." Dez listened to shuffling papers until Mark came back on the line.

"Okay, shoot."

"Her name is Shannon Perrault. She's sixteen, raised in foster care on the Island, and moved here about six months ago with her brother Alex. He's in a dorm at UBC and she's been staying at Evergreen House."

"How'd your girl handle the morgue?"

"It was tough, but she's okay." Dez let out a ragged breath. "We're heading over to UBC in a few minutes."

"Tell the brother I'd like him to drop by my office in the morning."

"Will do. Thanks for letting us break it to him first."

Dez hung up the phone just as Martine opened the door.

* * *

Dez and Martine made the trip to the University of British Columbia in silence. When they reached their destination, Dez pulled into the parking lot beside the Museum of Anthropology.

After they parked the Jeep, Dez got his pipe case out of the back seat and they headed across a grassy lawn to the large tent that served as a gathering place for Native students and visitors.

"I'll break the news to Alex first," Martine told Dez. "It'll be easier than telling him in front of a stranger."

"That's a good idea. I'll set up my case and be ready in case he wants to do a pipe ceremony."

Dez spread out his blanket and removed the smudge and pipe from his case. In the quiet spot beside the Longhouse, he sent a prayer out to the Creator that Shannon's killer would be caught quickly. He had been sitting for several minutes when Martine approached with a tall slender youth.

"Alex," she said, stopping in front of Dez, "this is my co-worker, Dez Pallaton,"

Dez held out his hand and Alex met his grip. Their eyes locked.

"Words won't help much right now." Dez let his sorrow show in his eyes. "I've brought my pipe. If you choose, we can ask the ancestors to help Shannon cross into the spirit world."

"I'd like that," Alex said, and his voice trembled slightly.

They sat on the ground in a partial circle and Dez took a bundle from his case. He removed a seashell, an eagle feather, a bag of sage and a bottle of powder.

"We'll cleanse our circle," he said, sprinkling sage into the seashell and striking a match. A small plume of smoke rose from the shell and Dez fanned it with the feather. When the smoke puffed into a cloud he put his hands into the smoke.

"Unclean spirits leave this circle." Dez commanded as he washed the smoke over his head and down his arms and legs.

Alex and Martine placed their hands into the smoke and repeated the cleansing ritual, both ordering unclean spirits to leave their circle.

When they had finished, Alex and Martine sat back while Dez opened his case and removed the pipe. He filled it with a mixture of herbs and natural tobacco then struck a match and started the smoke. Holding the stem to each of the four sacred directions Dez began to petition the Creator.

"Great Spirit. We offer this smoke in honor of our sister who is making her journey into the spirit world. Her brother is here, and he asks a special blessing for his young sister. My friend Martine and I join him in offering our prayers and asking you to protect this young sister on her journey into the spirit world."

They shared the pipe, passing it back and forth until the ashes died. When they finished, Dez emptied the bowl and replaced everything in his case.

"You have questions." Dez turned to Alex and invited the young man to speak.

"Do you know how she died?"

"Detective Mark Hanson of Vancouver Homicide called me at work this morning to say a Native girl had been murdered. He asked me to look at a picture. Of course, I didn't know your sister, so I didn't recognize her."

"Was she raped?" Pain distorted Alex's face, but he held onto his emotions.

Dez nodded. "I'm sorry. I'm afraid it wasn't an easy death."

"Do you think they'll catch the killer?"

"Hanson will do his best, but I'm afraid they may have the wrong idea. They found a Medicine Card on Shannon's body. That's got Hanson thinking the killer is Native. I believe he's wrong."

"Oh God. I hope it's not a brother. Will the cops listen to you?"

"I think so. I'm their liaison with Native youth. Of course, I'm not usually involved in murder, but I've done a few workshops with Hanson. He's a good cop and he's willing to consider every angle. He already has a Native detective consulting with him on this case, but Carver, that's the detective's name, is with the gang unit. He doesn't have the time for a murder case. The fact that your sister was a Native youth – and potentially a street-endangered youth, gives me the right to ask Hanson to let me become involved. I think he'll go along. At least I'm hoping."

"I appreciate that." Alex choked back a sob. "Will you let me know?"

"I'll talk to Hanson and call you later."

"Thanks. I'll wait by the phone."

* * *

Back in the truck Dez got out his cell and called Homicide. "Hi Mark. I've just come from speaking with Alex. He'll stop by the station in the morning, like we discussed. He doesn't know much though."

"Did you get anything worthwhile?"

"He hasn't spent a lot of time with his sister since they've been in Vancouver. He mentioned a place on Commercial Drive where she liked to hang out. There's a boyfriend, and maybe a bit of friction with the foster parents. I thought I'd check those out if it's okay with you."

"Go ahead. Just keep me informed. You know the lines."

"I will. Thanks Mark."

Dez pocketed his phone and turned to Martine. "You going back to the Friendship Centre?

"Yes, please. I want to tell the girls in my Circle about Shannon. I don't know how much time I'll need to spend with them, but I'd like to help you with your investigation."

"Sure. Any assistance will be welcome. I have a meeting this afternoon that's going to take up the rest of my day, but I'd like to pay a call on the housemother at Evergreen House first thing tomorrow morning. I'd

38

appreciate it if you'd call and clear it for me to go through Shannon's things."

"I'll call right now." Martine dug her cell phone out of her purse and punched in a number."

"Mrs. Lawrence. This is Martine LaChance. I've some sad news for you. We've found Shannon's body. She's been murdered."

Dez watched Martine while she listened as the older woman no doubt expressed her shock and horror. After several moments, Martine spoke again.

"Thank you. I'm going to tell the girls in her circle this morning. I'd also like to alert you that Mr. Pallaton, our Police Liaison, will be stopping by tomorrow morning to speak to your girls and check out Shannon's room. Alex, Shannon's brother, has given Mr. Pallaton permission to remove anything he needs in his investigation."

By the time Martine finished her conversation Dez had pulled up in front of the Friendship Center.

"Mrs. Lawrence will be expecting you," she said. "Will you let me know if you're able to find out anything?"

"Of course."

Martine thanked him and hopped out of the Jeep.

* * *

It was ten o'clock the next morning when Dez pulled up in front of a large Colonial with a wraparound front porch and pillars flanking the front door. He opened the screen and knocked sharply. A thin, gray-haired woman with sharp eyes behind round glasses and a tentative smile opened the door.

"Hello. I'm Dez Pallaton. Martine LaChance said you'd be expecting me."

"I'm Phyllis Lawrence. Come in." She opened the door wide.

"Girls," this is Mr. Pallaton." Mrs. Lawrence led Dez into a comfortably furnished parlor where three young girls sprawled on the floor in front of a television set.

"Hello ladies," Dez responded to a chorus of "Hi Mr. Pallaton."

"Mr. Pallaton is a police liaison officer. I'm taking him up to Shannon's room. He'll go through her things and later he might have some questions. You don't have to answer them if you don't want to, but it would be nice for Alex's sake. He really wants to find out who killed Shannon, as I'm sure you do."

"Thanks," Dez said when they reached Shannon's room.

"I spoke with Alex after Martine called. He asked me to allow you to look at and remove any of Shannon's things that might be helpful in your investigation."

"I'll tell you if I need to take anything."

"That's fine then," she said, stepping back from the door. "I just wanted you to know I'd spoken to Alex."

The room was long and narrow with a single bed under the dormer window and a mirrored dresser with a wooden chair and dressing table next to the bed. The bedcover had been hastily pulled over the pillows—Mrs. Lawrence's work Dez guessed. Makeup bottles and tubes, brushes, jars of cream, and tubes of lotion were scattered around the dresser tops, and clothes tossed over chairs and hanging on doorknobs.

Typical teen. Dez crouched in front of the dressing table and pulled out a drawer. After several minutes of sorting, he had a small stack of paper piled on Shannon's bed. His stash consisted of a couple of editorials about whale hunting in Clayoquot Sound, a picture of a pony-tailed youth holding a Save the Whales placard, and three drink napkins and match books—one from The Java Hut, one from a taxi company and one from The Fish House at Stanley Park.

A wire rack sitting on the desk held an unopened envelope addressed to Shannon Perrault. Mentally apologizing to the deceased, Dez picked up a letter opener and slit the seal. Holding it open he removed a cheque for $500.00 made out to Shannon and signed by Ed Parker. Could he be the foster father? Dez made a mental note to ask Alex. The envelope was postmarked April 9.

Shannon was killed Wednesday night. So, she'd had the check for a week.

I'd think cashing a $500.00 cheque would be right at the top of a teenage girl's priorities. I'll let Mrs. Lawrence know I'm taking it to Alex. We'll see what he knows about this Ed Parker.

An hour of searching turned up nothing more of interest. Dez put the envelope and the brochure in his jacket pocket and left the room.

Downstairs he waited at the doorway to the parlor while the credits for The Young and The Restless flashed across the screen. The girls were on the floor in front of the television. They lay, chins propped in hands, with six legs swinging choreographed kicks. When the show switched to commercials Dez spoke.

"Hi ladies. Anyone up for questions?"

Three heads swung to focus questioning eyes on Dez.

"I promise I don't bite." He smiled and showed his teeth.

"I'm Amy Grant." A chubby redhead stood up and matched his smile with a tentative one of her own. "We decided I should be the one to answer questions since I knew Shannon best." She motioned to the other girls who nodded their agreement.

"Sounds great. How about we go back up to Shannon's room. Is that okay?"

Amy followed Dez up the stairs. "I can sit here," she said, perching on the side of the bed and leaving the chair for Dez.

"Thank you, Amy. I appreciate you talking to me. Perhaps you can tell me about Shannon from a friend's viewpoint. I've talked to Alex, but he's her brother. Brothers see their sisters differently than friends. Friends usually know them better."

"I guess." Amy frowned. "Shannon was kind of funny."

"Funny?"

"Yeah. She didn't socialize with the girls much. She didn't like people 'getting into her business'. That's how she used to put it."

"But she liked you?"

"Well. I don't know if she liked me that much. She needed somebody to keep her up with stuff and cover for her, sort of. I guess she kind of tolerated me."

Dez smiled. "I'm sure it was more than that. So how did Shannon spend her free time, do you know that?"

Amy looked up at him with a troubled expression in her eyes. She seemed to be debating something.

"I'm sure you're worried about telling Shannon's secrets. I know I would be if it was my friend. But somebody murdered her. She was your friend and keeping secrets might just be helping her killer, not Shannon. You don't want that, do you?"

Amy bowed her head and Dez leaned forward, watching her face. She lifted her eyes to meet his gaze and tears blinked on her lashes. "No," she whispered. "I don't want that."

"Did Shannon have some secrets that might be considered bad? Is that what you're afraid of telling?"

"I feel so awful." Amy's voice broke into a sob.

"Don't feel bad. You can tell me, Amy. I promise I won't tell anyone unless it involves the killer, and then I'll protect Shannon as much as I can." Dez reached out and patted her hand.

"Shannon slept with men for money," Amy blurted.

"I see." Dez noted the frightened look on Amy's face. "It's okay, Amy. You can tell me what you know."

"I'm sorry," she sobbed. "It's just that I don't want people to think bad things about Shannon because I told."

"They won't. Someone murdered Shannon. What you're telling me could make the difference between us catching her killer or his getting away with murder."

She pulled a tissue out of the box on Shannon's dressing table, blew her nose, and turned her attention back to Dez. "I'm okay now."

"Good. Now were there many men, or was it one particular man?"

"I don't know. Shannon liked to exaggerate sometimes. She'd say things just to see how I'd react. But she did meet someone last Monday, because I saw him."

"You did? This is important, Amy. No one has seen Shannon since Monday night, so the man you saw her with may have been the killer, or at least the last person to see her alive."

"No, I saw her Tuesday morning. She snuck in to change her clothes and she asked me not to tell anyone."

"When was this?"

"Just before lunch time, maybe 11:30. I had a cold, so I skipped my morning class. I was lying in bed when someone knocked on my window."

"Your window? Up here?"

"There's a ladder at the back. If you climb to the first floor roof you can come right around to our bedroom window. We use it sometimes. You won't tell Mrs. Lawrence?"

"That doesn't seem terribly safe, Amy. You might want to think about telling her yourself."

"Okay. I guess I will," she muttered unconvincingly.

"So, Shannon knocked on the window and you let her in. What did she say?"

"She said she needed to change clothes and she didn't want the Dragon—that's what she called Mrs. Lawrence—to catch her."

"I see," Dez stifled a chuckle. "I take it Shannon didn't get along with your housemother."

"Shannon didn't like the way she stuck her nose into our business. I think she liked her okay, except for that."

"Now about this man you say she met on Monday. Did you see him?"

"Yes. I wasn't sure if she was really meeting someone or if she was making it up, so I followed her. She walked down Commercial to Hastings until a cab pulled up next to her and this Native guy got out. He opened the back door for Shannon and she jumped in. Shannon would kill me for telling this," she muttered and then stopped as if remembering that Shannon wouldn't be killing anyone.

"It's okay, Amy. Shannon would understand. What did he look like?"

"Hot." She lifted her head and met Dez's eyes. "Shoulder length black hair, tall, sexy butt. He looked like somebody important."

"How's that?"

"The way he was dressed. Not a suit, but slacks, nice sweater, the kind of stuff my dad wears. Not like most of the guys around here."

"Anything stand out about him?"

"Just that he was a hunk."

"Was he Caucasian, or do you think he was native, like me?"

"Jeez, I really can't be sure."

Dez grinned. "Okay. Thanks Amy. You've been very helpful." He opened the door, so she could precede him down the stairs. "Is it okay to call you if I have more questions?"

"Sure." A smile playing across Amy's lips as she rushed down the stairs to join her friends and tell them what she'd learned.

Chapter Three

Back in the Jeep, Dez dialed Phil's number.

"Yo," Phil answered on the first buzz. "Hey, just wondering if I could stop by and run a problem we've run into by you and maybe you could take it up with your friend Wisdomkeeper?"

"As a matter of fact I'm headed out to Wisdomkeeper's cabin this afternoon. We've got some ceremonial work we want to collaborate on so I'll be out there for a couple of days. If you remember where it is from last summer, you're welcome to stop by and we'll both give your problem a listen and see if we might be able to help."

"That would be great. If it's okay with you I'd like to bring along my friend Martine. We're both kind of involved in this situation so I think it will be helpful if you hear the story from both of us."

"You'll both be welcome. If we're not at the cabin when you get there just go ahead on in and make yourselves comfortable. We'll be nearby and will be back as soon as we've finished with some work we'll be doing."

Dez hung up the phone and punched in Martine's number. He got her voicemail and left a message that he was headed back to the Friendship Centre. Once there he left a note in Martine's inbox that he'd talked to Phil who told him that he'd be out at the cabin with Wisdomkeeper for a couple of days and if they wanted to talk to them about their current problem, they'd be welcome out there.

At his desk, Dez started on the paperwork that had piled up and moved a couple of appointments to the next week.

An hour had passed when Martine poked her head in his doorway. "Sorry it took me so long. I'd love to go with you if the offer's still open."

"Sounds good. Give me five and I'll meet you out at the Jeep."

* * *

"Wisdomkeeper is kind of a loner," Dez said, breaking the silence they'd graciously maintained while he manipulated Vancouver's urban congestion and crossed the bridge to Highway 1 headed toward Hope. "He lives in a log cabin built about forty years ago and he doesn't have a telephone."

"Sounds intriguing."

"Oh, he is that." Dez's voice held a hint of laughter, "he and Phil make quite a team. You remember Phil, don't you? He did a

49

couple of presentations at the Friendship Center."

"Of course. He actually held a circle with my girls about six months ago. He might even remember Shannon. I'm glad he's going to be there."

As they sped along the highway, Dez watched for landmarks and when he recognized the nearly hidden road snaking off the right shoulder into the trees. He made a sharp turn and told Martine that she had better hang on," as he steered the Jeep onto little more than a trail meandering through the grasses. They bumped and jolted along a pair of ruts, hitting potholes and stubborn roots that bounced them to the roof.

"The rest of us may be part of the twentieth century," Dez said, after dropping a tire to the axle in a mud puddle far deeper than it looked had them both rubbing the top of their heads, "but Wisdomkeeper still heats his cabin with wood and fetches his water from a well."

"We have a few old timers like that around Montreal." Martine smiled. "Who's to say they aren't living better than the rest of us."

"That's a fact." Dez agreed. "We're in luck, there's smoke coming from the chimney so it looks like Phil made it out here and... yup, that looks like him and Wisdomkeeper sitting on the porch."

Dez braked in front of an old, weathered cabin. "Here we are." He opened the door and stepped out of the Jeep. Martine jumped out of her side and met him in front. "These steps are a bit rough," he said, taking her hand and guiding her toward a stack of rough-hewn logs that served for a staircase.

"Thanks." She followed him up, then freed her hand and ran her fingers along the bark railing circling the porch. Fashioned from willow and twisted into a braid, the wood had been aged by decades in the elements. Oversized chairs woven from the same willows circled a metal fire pit.

A tall, straight-backed Native man rose from one of the chairs. Silver-streaked black hair flowed over his shoulders and coal black eyes measured the young couple as they approached.

"Dez Pallaton. You have brought a friend?"

"This is Martine. She's the Family Response Worker at the Friendship Centre."

"Ah, you maybe know my friend," Wisdomkeeper pointed to Phil.

"All acquainted," Phil said. "How are you, Martine? I hope all your girls are doing well."

Martine held her hand out and Phil took it in both of his. "No," he said. "Something is not right."

Martine shook her head and tears threatened her eyes. "Do you remember

Shannon, she's the one from the Island who followed her brother here?"

"Yes, of course. A quiet girl with troubled brown eyes. I spoke to her a little but she seemed to be holding back and I wondered if she might be hiding something."

"She's dead." Martine's voice broke, but she held Phil's eyes and continued. "That's why we're here. Dez has a copy of a Medicine Card the police found at the scene and he's hoping you and Wisdomkeeper might be able to understand the meaning."

Wisdomkeeper and Dez had been standing quietly listening to Phil and Martine, but Dez reached in his pocket and took out the photocopy of the card.

"This is it," he said handing it across to Wisdomkeeper.

"Something very bad has happened." Wisdomkeeper spoke softly holding the picture high so Phil could see it as well.

"The cops found a Native girl raped and murdered in Stanley Park. We've discovered that she was one of the girls Martine looks after at Evergreen House, and the police think she was killed by one of our brothers."

"And you do not believe this?"

"No. My gut tells me the killer is a white man posing as an Indian. I've convinced Mark Hanson to let me explore that theory. He doesn't agree, but he wants to catch the killer before there's another murder so he's willing to consider any possibility."

"You think there will be more of these killings?"

"Hanson thinks they're the work of a psychopath. If he's right, then we're dealing with a predator. Once he's tasted blood he won't stop until someone makes him."

"Are you sure it isn't a brother? You know the drugs have turned a lot of our people into animals."

"I know, but this girl wasn't just raped and murdered, she was defiled. The killer strangled her and then spread eagled her and stabbed a medicine card to her breast."

"Not a Brother then." Wisdomkeeper's eyes flashed. "To rape and kill the girl, this I could believe, but to anger the spirits, no. Even an Indian turned jackal would fear the spirit world."

Dez nodded and waited while Wisdomkeeper studied the picture. "The snake. Someone has angered a powerful spirit." He handed the picture across to Phil.

"Can you help us?"

"Wait while I get my case. We'll go up the mountain."

* * *

They climbed high, to an old burial ground where centuries ago Native men and women buried their dead. Abandoned by a new generation the grasses grew tall and brittle, gravestones crumbled into the earth. At the entrance Phil and Wisdomkeeper motioned them to stop while they stepped up to the gate. Removing their pipes, they chanted an ancient language as they lifted the pipe stems to each of the four sacred directions. Finished, they motioned for Dez and Martine to join them.

"We have asked the ancestors to gather," Phil said. "We will light our smudge and wait."

A white mist drifted up from the river below and clouds caught by gusts of wind danced in the clearing. Seated Indian style, facing Phil and Wisdomkeeper, Dez and Martine watched twigs catch fire and curl into smoke.

Phil bent to the fire, scooped a handful of smoke and washed it down his arms and legs. He spoke a warning to uninvited spirits. "Unclean ones leave us now, you are not welcome inside this circle."

Wisdomkeeper and then Dez and Martine reached into the smoke to cleanse themselves.

"The Spirits are close." Wisdomkeeper passed the stem of his pipe to Dez, then turned to Phil. "We are ready."

Phil stood and raised his hands. "Thank you, Great Spirit. We come to ask for guidance from the spirit world."

Time passed. They shared the pipe and took their turns offering prayers. The white mist filling the circle turned grey and then to black. Darkness filled the graveyard.

"What's happening?" Martine whispered.

Light flooded the circle and a skittering sound broke the silence. A white rabbit hopped into the circle and the two Elders started a chant. The rabbit froze as if mesmerized. The light spilled over the rabbit's fur giving it an ephemeral glow. The animal glowed for several minutes before it darted out of the clearing.

Phil and Wisdomkeeper continued their chant.

An owl swooped down into the circle and snatched a mouse. Rodent blood dripped from its beak. The bird flew away. Dez nudged Martine and pointed to where a coyote with blood red eyes crouched behind a gravestone

The light faded and plunged the circle into darkness.

They ceased their chant.

"Did you see the same thing I did?" Martine asked Dez.

"I think so." He turned to the two Elders. "Do you know what all that meant?"

They paused in the act of packing their cases. "It is to you that the Spirits have given a message. It is you who must seek their meaning."

* * *

"What did you make of that scene with the rabbit?" Martine asked when they were back in the truck.

"I've been thinking back to what the grandfathers say about the spirit world. The way the rabbit glowed, it could be a message telling us our petitions at the pipe ceremony were honored and Shannon has crossed into the spirit world. The rabbit did remind me of an angel the way the light sort of *haloed* above it." Martine nodded agreement with his theory, then turned to him with another question, "what about the owl and the mouse?"

"I think I know what that means but you might not want to hear my theory."

"Why? What are you thinking!"

"That the owl with the bloody mouse in its beak is a warning that there's going to be another killing."

"Oh God, I hope not. It makes me sick to think about another girl being killed."

"I feel the same, but it's the only thing I can come up with that makes sense of that vision.

"What about the coyote?"

"Coyote is known as the trickster—the dual sided one, so following that analogy, the killer could be someone we know or someone we meet who is not what he, or she, seems."

Martine, who had been watching him with widened eyes, shuddered. "That would fit the profile of a psychopath, they're seldom what they seem, you know. Remember Ted Bundy?"

"Who doesn't? He's one of Seattle's most infamous sons."

"And yet, everyone who knew him swore they'd never met a nicer guy."

"Excluding those girls who tried to help him. Sick bastard."

"I know. It's sad really, he's become kind of a local legend. I hate to think there might be someone like that targeting our Native girls."

"Local freak is more accurate. I hate it too, but at this point it's the only thing that makes sense."

"Where will you even start to look for that kind of killer?"

"Probably with Shannon, I need to do some digging into her background."

"Alex said Shannon liked to hang around with New Age kids. He mentioned a coffee house they use for a hangout"

"That's right, I remember that now, the Java Hut, wasn't it?"

"Yah, that's the place. It's over on Commercial Drive, not far from our condo, actually."

"Good, maybe I'll drop in there after I've had a talk with Hanson."

"Why don't you let me handle that? It's been a while, but with some makeup magic and the right wardrobe I think I could pass for a teenager."

Dez opened his mouth to speak, and then wisely closed it again. Martine would not appreciate overbearing protectivity from him. She wanted to do her part.

* * *

Martine studied her reflection in the bathroom mirror and pouted her lips to apply a coat of dark red lipstick. Her black hair hung straight, and with an iron she'd fashioned a pair of downward-pointing spikes at her temples. She'd coated her face with white pancake, lined her eyes with black kohl, and sprinkled silver sparkles over her gaudy purple lashes.

"My God," she groaned, "I look like Morticia Addams."

Makeup finished, she pulled on a pair of fishnet stockings, zipped up her black leather mini and laced her feet into worn black combat boots.

Giving herself a last minute once-over in the mirror, Martine picked up her bag and let herself out of the apartment.

At the Java Hut she pulled open the door and stood inside, getting her bearings. There were a few couples seated at tables and two people seated at the bar. Martine walked up to a young girl and pulled out a stool. "You a regular?" She asked.

The girl, thin with orange blonde hair, tilted her head to meet Martine's eyes.

58

"Why?" Her bright red lips parted to show a double row of metal braces.

"I'm looking for my cousin. Her brother said she hangs out here."

"What's her name?"

"Shannon. Shannon Perrault."

"Sure, I know Shannon. Haven't seen her for a while. What's your name?"

"Martine. You?"

"Diana. You from around here?"

"The Island. I'm at a reunion thing— bo-r-ring. I figured to find Shannon and hang out."

"Les. Over here." Diana called out to a skinny boy with green hair who'd just walked in the front door. "If anyone knows where to find Shannon it's Les," she said when the young man joined them at the bar.

"Hey D, whats up?" He stopped in front of Martine and looked her up and down.

"Hi yourself." Martine met the young man's gaze and held it for several seconds.

"Shannon's been holding out on us." Les leaned against the bar beside Martine.

"Do you know Shannon?"

"We're what you might call friends."

Diana tossed her head and laughed. "They're a bit more than friends. Where have you been all week?" She turned back to Les.

"The Island. Why? What's it to you?"

"Don't be touchy. Martine's a cousin of Shannon's. I figured since the two of you were such a hot item you'd know where to find her."

"Nope. Haven't seen her." He turned to Martine and smiled again. "Diana's got too much mouth. Shannon and I called it quits a couple weeks ago —by mutual agreement. I've been on the Island—trying to save the old-growth from a bunch of parasite developers."

"Any idea where Shannon's been staying? Her brother hasn't seen her since Monday."

"Sorry. I got no idea." Les shrugged. "She'll turn up. Maybe you'd like to come to a project meeting tomorrow night? Shannon's a supporter. She'll probably show."

"Where are you meeting?"

"We have a house behind the Britannia Recreation Centre. Tell the receptionist at Britannia you're part of Eugene Guthrie's group. She'll point you in the right direction."

"Thanks. I'll see how it goes. Nice meeting you, Diana." Martine slid off her stool and waved at the couple as she headed out the door.

"Nice meeting you." Diana called back.

Chapter Four

Once inside her condo Martine went straight to the shower. After scrubbing all the paint off her face and changing into jeans she grabbed a loose knit sweater, tossed it over her shoulder and headed for Dez's place.

She knocked softly and waited until she heard a muffled, "come in."

Walking through the condo, an inverted duplicate of her own, Martine heard the sounds of running water and headed for the bedroom.

"Are you decent?" She poked her head through the doorway and scanned the dimly lit room.

"Depends." Dez stepped out of the bathroom sporting a towel wrapped loosely around his waist and lots of bare brown skin. Water drops glistened on his flat belly and strands of jet-black hair clung to his shoulders.

A sizzling current zipped through Martine's belly. "Sorry, I'll wait outside."

"No, don't go. Hand me those pants on the bed. I want to hear about your trip to Java House."

Martine grabbed the pair of well-worn Levis off the bed.

"Here." She stepped to the bathroom and held them out.

Dez's fingers covered hers.

"Hey, we're still on the clock," she said, "you know the rules."

"You can turn around now." His voice whispered against her earlobe. "Why don't we sit?"

Martine shook her head. "I love my job and I don't want anything to change."

"I understand. Speaking of the job, want to take a ride?"

"Have you found out something?"

"I'm not sure, but there are a couple of curiosities I want to check out." He reached into his pocket and pulled out Ed Parker's cheque. "This is one of them."

Martine took the cheque and read the signature "That's Shannon's foster father. I wonder why he would give her a cheque. From what Alex said they were barely on speaking terms."

"Exactly, so why would Parker give her five hundred dollars?"

Martine shook her head. "I have no idea, but I can see why you'd find it curious."

"Yes, and then there's this." Dez pulled out a matchbook and napkin. "According to Amy, one of Shannon's roommates, she met a man Monday night."

"I take it you mean someone older than her boyfriend from the Java Hut."

"According to Amy, Shannon told her that men paid for her company, but Amy wasn't sure if Shannon was telling the truth. Apparently, Shannon liked to embellish her exploits a good deal."

"Poor Alex, I hope it isn't true."

"I know, but we'll need to find out. Meantime, do you mind if we stop by the Fish House?"

"Not at all, in fact, I'm really hungry." Martine slanted a look in Dez's direction, but he wisely refrained from comment.

"Good. We can kill two birds, as they say, get some food and quiz the wait staff. I'm not too optimistic, there are a lot of tourists visiting the Fish House this time of year, so finding someone who remembers one particular couple will be a long shot."

Martine grinned. "Since we have to eat anyway, it's worth a try."

"Sold." Dez opened the door of the condo for Martine to pass through and followed her down to the Jeep.

"Would you like to drive?" Dez held out the keys, "that way we can stop at UBC and I can hop out and go show Alex this cheque while you circle around with the truck. We might get lucky and grab a parking spot, but you never can tell- parking can be hell over there."

"Sure, and thanks, I'd love to drive." Martine buckled herself into the driver's seat, set the GPS for UBC, and pulled smoothly into traffic.

Dez took out his cell phone and selected Alex's number. His sleepy voice answered on the third ring.

"Alex? This is Dez. Did I wake you?" Dez asked, guessing he'd caught the young man still in bed.

"It's okay. I need to be up anyhow. I've got exams this week and I studied most of the night. Is there news?"

"I have a couple of questions. Can you spare fifteen minutes?"

"Sure, as long as you mean like right now. Got class at noon."

"I'll be there in ten minutes."

Dez hit the call end button and turned to Martine. "If you go around to the museum of anthropology side, you can pull into the drop off zone and I'll cut through the path behind the longhouse. You can probably sit there and keep the jeep running, I won't be long. If the parking patrol comes along just tell them you're picking up a facilitator. I do programs here all the time, so they might recognize the jeep anyhow."

"Sure. I'm glad you've shown me this area. When I come over to do circles, I drive myself crazy trying to find parking. I'm going to remember this lot in the future."

"It's expensive – like everything else over here – but at least it's easy in and out and there's usually room in the lot."

At the museum, Dez jumped out and Martine pulled up under a spreading maple tree. Dez took off down a narrow pathway loosely strewn with brush and brambles and made his way to Alex's section of student housing.

Alex came walking out the doorway of his building just as Dez started up the steps.

"I figured I'd meet you out here and save you the climb." The young man offered his hand and a grin.

"Thanks," Dez chuckled. "I guess my years are showing. I wonder if you know anything about this." He handed over Ed Parker's $500.00 cheque.

Alex took the cheque, looked at the signature and did a double take. "That's our foster dad. But I sure don't know why he'd give Shannon a cheque for $500.00."

"Could he be paying her tuition?"

"I don't believe it. Ed wasn't exactly a fan of Shannon's, especially after she ran away from the Island. No way he'd give her $500.00 for tuition."

"Okay, so that's something I need to find out."

"Do you want me to call him?"

"No. I'm planning a trip over to the Island this weekend. If you don't mind, I'd just as soon drop in unannounced."

"That suits me. I called Mina, my foster mom, to tell her about Shannon. She didn't mention Ed and I didn't ask."

"I also found this." Dez held up the Fish House matchbook cover. "I don't suppose Shannon mentioned this place?"

Alex shook his head. "That's not Shannon's type of restaurant."

"She probably just picked it up somewhere." Dez put the cheque and matchbook back in his pocket.

"I wish I could be more help."

"No sweat. I'm just looking for inconsistencies. Most of this stuff is meaningless, just details that don't quite fit the picture. I'll call you when I get back from the Island. If you think of anything, give me a call. I'll have my cell."

"Thanks. I appreciate it."

* * *

"How's he doing?" Martine asked when Dez got back in the truck.

"He's okay," Dez replied, "busy with exams."

"That's good, it'll keep him from worrying. Did he know anything about the cheque?"

"No. He was mystified. He said there wasn't any love lost between Shannon and Ed Parker and he couldn't think of a single reason why Parker would give her money."

"Even before this happened, I wondered about Shannon's relationship with her foster family. She never talked about them and if anyone questioned her about life on the Island, she'd brush it off."

"I have an idea," Dez said, fastening his seatbelt and turning in his seat to face Martine.

"What's that?"

"Didn't you say you'd like to visit Vancouver Island?" Dez fixed an innocent grin on his face.

"It's at the top of my 'must do' list."

"Since Shannon's foster parents live in Victoria, I figured we might take a kind of working holiday."

"Sounds great, but right now I'm hungry."

"Okay let's get to the Fish House. Traffic gets a little dodgy around the Park this time of day and I know a short cut or two."

"Wonderful. I didn't want to complain, but if you'd taken much longer, that century old pack of crackers you have in the glovebox might have been history."

Dez jumped out of the cab and headed for the driver's door while Martine slid into the passenger seat.

"Let's get this show on the road," he said. "Starving women scare me to death."

* * *

Entering the Park on the English Bay side, Dez drove along Stanley Park Drive giving Martine an opportunity to take in the spectacular gardens.

"I've heard so much about this park, but actually driving through gives you a whole different perspective."

"That's the Fish House." Dez pointed to a genteel old mansion perched in the center of an enormous plantation style garden.

"Wow."

"It's a huge tourist attraction. Fortunately, it's late for lunch so we should be able to find parking. It gets dicey around dinnertime. How about that, front row." Dez swung the Jeep into a spot near the front steps and turned off the ignition.

"Do you have the photos Alex gave us earlier?"

"Yes, right here." Martine took one of the pictures of Alex and Shannon out of her purse. "According to Alex this one is the most recent."

"Good. We'll order and then I'll do some asking around."

After a short wait, the hostess led them to a table for two overlooking the gardens. "You wouldn't happen to recognize this couple?" Dez asked holding the picture up for the girl to see.

"Sorry. Neither one of them looks familiar." She shook her head and motioned to a gangly young man in his late twenties who trotted over with menus.

"The special today is cedar planked salmon," he said, as he filled their water glasses.

"Sounds good." Dez looked at Martine and she nodded agreement.

"I'll have the same," she said.

"Excellent," the youth jotted their orders in his book and retrieved the menus. "Are you visiting our city?"

"No, we're locals," Dez replied. "As a matter of fact, we're hoping you might recognize someone." He held up the picture of Shannon and Alex. "Do you remember seeing the girl anytime within the past two weeks?"

The youth looked at the picture and frowned. "She looks familiar, but our clientele is mainly tourists. We don't usually see the same people more than once or twice, so it's hard to remember any particular person."

"Yes, I kind of figured that. It's a long shot, but if you'd take a good look, we'd apprcciatc your hclp. The girl was murdered this past week. The man in the picture is her brother. Of course, the police are looking into everything but Alex, that's her brother, asked us to try and retrace her steps last week."

"That's pretty rotten. The more I look at the picture, the more she looks like a girl that came in here last week with a well-dressed native man. I was off on Sunday, so if it's the right couple they were here Monday night. They had a reservation for six and he paid with a government credit card."

"Any chance I could take a look at your reservation book?"

"Gosh, I don't think I can do that. We're not supposed to give out personal information on customers." The young man looked over his shoulder and then back at Dez. "I'd like to help, but I could lose my job."

"That's okay," Dez smiled and held out his hand. "There's no need for you to risk your job. I'll tell the detective in charge of the case that Shannon might have been here on Monday night. He'll come in officially and look at the reservation book. He will question you, along with the rest of the staff, and you can tell him what you've told me, but he won't single you out."

"Thanks. I appreciate that. I hope they find the creep that killed her. I've got a sister too and I know how I'd feel."

"I'll let Mark know," Dez made a quick call on his cell phone, then settled down to enjoy the excellent salmon.

"Mark's got a car on its way over here," he said, after he'd paid the bill and they headed back to the Jeep. "They'll check out the reservation book and by the time we're back at the Friendship Center he'll probably know all about the mysterious Native guy who took Shannon out to dinner the night before she died."

"I guess the cops could be right about the killer being Native."

"Maybe, depends on what this guy has to say for himself."

"I'm just worried about how Alex will feel if his sister was murdered by one of her own people."

"I guess we've done all we can for today. Did you want to go home or were you going back to work?"

"Work please. I've been letting things pile up the last couple days. I'll need to burn some midnight oil tonight."

Dez dropped Martine at the entrance to the Friendship Center and headed for Vancouver Homicide. He wanted to clear his trip to Victoria with Mark, and then he planned to head home to make reservations.

Chapter Five

"All set?" Dez asked when Martine answered his knock the next morning.

"I'm just about finished. I worked until after midnight last night, so I'm moving kind of slow. Would you like some coffee?

"Thanks. I brought my own." Dez held up a Starbucks cup. "It looks like we're going to have a great day for crossing the Strait of Georgia. We might even spot some killer whales."

"That would be a treat!." Martine spoke from the open door of her bedroom where she had bent over to add a few more items to her suitcase.

"On another note," Dez said to her back. "I just got off the phone with Hanson. He had some interesting news."

"About Shannon's killer?"

"Her escort. I'm not convinced he's our killer. The guy's name is Lyle Miller. He's a statistician for Indian Affairs in Ottawa. He's been in town working on a federal aid program the government is set to roll out to the Bands. Miller is married, and he is not anxious for his wife to find out about his dinner with Shannon."

"He should be more concerned about the fact that Shannon was only sixteen than whether or not his wife finds out that he's been playing around."

"He swears Shannon told him she was nineteen and Hanson is inclined to believe his story. According to Hanson, Miller didn't even try to dodge questions. He came clean immediately."

"That's in his favor."

"It is. Miller met Shannon at the downtown library on Monday afternoon. She told him she was a student at UBC doing research for a term paper on Native culture."

"That sounds credible. Shannon skipped my Monday afternoon circle. If this Miller is telling the truth that would explain why she didn't show up."

"Miller claims they talked for a couple of hours and he invited her to dinner."

"So how did Amy see him outside of Evergreen house?"

"Shannon told Miller she had to tutor a student at Evergreen House. He dropped her off in a cab, then kept an appointment of his own and picked her up two hours later on the corner of Hastings and Commercial."

"I'm surprised Mark hasn't arrested him given the fact that he's admitted spending the evening with her."

"That might happen yet. Mark's under a lot of pressure to make an arrest."

"If I were Lyle, I'd get in touch with a good lawyer."

"Apparently that's already been done, and I know Mark himself has doubts about Miller's guilt. He actually seemed optimistic when I told him I was following up a lead concerning Shannon's foster father who lives on Vancouver Island."

* * *

"This is awesome," Martine leaned over the ferry's rail and watched the Spirit of Vancouver Island pull away from the pier.

"Have you ever ridden a ferry?"

"No. I've wanted to, but I never seemed to find the time."

"I'm glad to be along for your first." Dez brushed a strand of hair out of her face and let his hand linger on her shoulder.

Martine met his eyes, then turned back to the water. "How long before we have to go below deck?"

"The trip takes an hour and twenty minutes. They'll signal a return to vehicles about 15 minutes before docking."

"Let's go up top."

"It's pretty windy."

"I don't care. I've never had a chance to look for whales. A minute ago, a woman told me she saw a whole pod of them her last trip. They haven't seen anything today, but there are dolphins following the ship."

"Well then, let's get up there. Maybe we'll have better luck."

74

Unfortunately, the whales failed to make an appearance, but the breathtaking coastline, intricate waterways, small islands, and numerous attractive bays and coves kept them so enthralled they nearly missed the call to return to the departure deck.

A short shuttle ride brought them to downtown Victoria, where they entered a picturesque harbor teaming with sailboats that glided in and out of the docks. Martine's first sight of the Empress Hotel and the Parliament Buildings had her pressing her nose against the window.

"Look, over there." Martine drew Dez's attention to a horse drawn carriage crossing the intersection "and over there," she continued, grabbing his sleeve and pointing toward a double-decker bus. "I'd love to ride one of them."

"Maybe we can take a tour. I think that one's headed over to the House of Parliament."

"It's beautiful, and the Empress Hotel. I can't wait to see the inside. I've heard it's practically a palace."

"Then you'll be happy to know that's where we're staying."

"Isn't it terribly expensive?"

"Worth it. Besides, we get a government rate. I've booked a suite since I used both of our accounts."

* * *

"What an absolutely perfect night." Martine's eyes sparkled as she stood in the living room of their decidedly Victorian suite. "This hotel is gorgeous, and the food at the Blue Crab was out of this world. How did you manage to find that place?"

"The Director suggested it. I'll have to thank her."

"I'm so full I can hardly move, and exhausted too. What do you have planned for morning?"

"I'm hoping to see the Parkers first thing. You're welcome to come along, but if you'd like to do a bit of sight-seeing, please go ahead."

"Thank you. I would like to see a bit of the city. If you're sure you don't need my help, I'll probably take one of the tours they have listed down in the lobby."

"Sound great. How about if we meet back here for high tea? From what I've heard it's a 'not to be missed' experience."

"High tea! Its like we're stuck in some alternate time loop."

Chapter Six

Saturday morning Dez climbed the steps of the two-bedroom ranch at 911 Lotus Street and knocked. Moments later, a mousy little woman with dishwater blond hair opened the door an inch and peered through the crack.

"Can I help you?"

"I'm looking for Mr. and Mrs. Ed Parker." Dez smiled to allay her unease. "It's in regard to their foster children Shannon and Alex."

She opened the door and looked quizzically up at Dez. "I'm Mrs. Parker. What about the children?"

Dez smiled again. Mention of the two young people had given her curiosity the upper hand. Mrs. Parker still thought of them as children. Her motherly instincts overrode any fears she might have about talking to a tall, unannounced stranger.

"My name is Dez Pallaton. I'm assisting Alex with some inquiries regarding Shannon's death. I know it must be hard for you to talk about the death of your foster daughter, but I'd appreciate any help you can give me."

"Please come inside." She stepped back and allowed him to pass through the open doorway. "Would you like some coffee?"

"That would be great." Dez followed her into a neat and tidy kitchen. She motioned him to a seat in one of the straight back chairs pulled up to a small table covered with a bright yellow cloth.

"I'm afraid we haven't heard from Shannon since she left here last year. Alex has probably told you that things were strained between us." She set two cups on the table, picked up a pot from the stove and filled them both.

"Alex suggested his foster dad might have visited Shannon on one of his trips to the mainland."

Mrs. Parker lifted her cup and drank. After a moment of silence, she shook her head. "I don't think so. Ed was very angry when Shannon left."

"So I understand. I was wondering though: Is it possible your husband decided to try reconciliation without telling anyone in case it didn't pan out?"

She tilted her head and stared at a spot over Dez's shoulder. "It's possible I suppose. Ed wouldn't like being rebuffed. Even so, once he's gotten down on someone, I've never known him to change his mind."

"Would it be possible for me to speak with Mr. Parker?"

"He's at a pool tournament today. He'll be out until late."

"Maybe I could stop by the tournament?"

The woman frowned and twisted the dishtowel in her hand. Her subservient relationship to her husband was evident in her demeanor.

"Alex is devastated over Shannon's death." Dez appealed to those motherly instincts again. "Perhaps Alex would know the spot where your husband is attending this tournament?"

"Ed's been going there for years." The frown creasing her brow cleared and Dez saw that she'd figured out his meaning.

"Why don't I just drop by there and wait for an opportunity to question your husband. I'll make it a point to mention that Alex suggested I might find him there."

"He'll be at Diego's over on Douglas Street." She had no hesitation about revealing Ed Parker's whereabouts once she knew Dez would name Alex as his source.

"I'll tell Alex how much you've helped." Dez smiled and pushed back his chair. "I doubt your husband will have any helpful information, but it'll make Alex feel better to know I've checked with everyone who might know something."

Located next door to the Red Lion Inn, Diego's had all the trappings of a popular sports bar with a number of strategically placed television sets and a large crowd clustered around three regulation pool tables.

Dez chose a spot at the bar that afforded a view of the tables. When a bartender finally strolled over, Dez ordered a beer.

"Looks like you have a tournament going on," Dez said when the man returned with his beer.

"Yep. Just a local affair, but we get a nice crowd."

"A friend asked me to look up his foster dad. He gave me a description, but I didn't anticipate a crowd like this."

"Anyone I might know?"

"Fellow by the name of Ed Parker."

"Oh sure. Everyone knows Ed. He's in the tournament. That's him next to the shooter, wearing the Budweiser T-shirt. They'll break in about half an hour. I can steer him your way if you like."

"That would be great. I'll get a table and grab a sandwich while I'm waiting."

Fifteen minutes later, during which Dez had time to put down a decent club sandwich, an average size balding guy with a bit of a potbelly pulled out a chair and settled into the seat across the table. "I hear you've been looking for me."

"You must be Ed Parker," Dez stuck out his hand. "I'm Dez Pallaton. I got your name from Alex."

"So I hear." Parker said, giving Dez's hand a brief shake. "Something I can do for you?"

"It's about Shannon."

"What about her? She ran away to the city. Got in over her head. Now she's dead. End of story." Parker scowled at some distant point over Dez's left shoulder.

"Sounds like you still have some issues."

Parker's face flushed. "What's it to you?" He shoved his chair back and fixed Dez with a belligerent glare.

"Take it easy," Dez said, reaching in his pocket and pulling out the $500.00 cheque. "Alex asked me to go through Shannon's belongings looking for clues related to her murder. I found this cheque and we decided I should come talk to you before turning it over to the police."

"Since when do the cops care about me giving one of my kids money?"

Dez shifted in his chair, stretched his legs and took a drink from his beer. Then he set the mug down and glanced across at Parker. There were beads of sweat standing out on the older man's bald head and his color did not look healthy. "It's common knowledge that the two of you have been estranged for more than a year. I'd think an unexpected five hundred dollar payment would call for an explanation."

"Yeah. Well maybe I'm not as hard-hearted as some people would like to think. Shannon called a couple of weeks ago. Said she was having a hard time, so I sent her a cheque," Parker said with a scowl.

"Any idea why she never cashed it?"

"No. I don't know a damn thing more than what I've just told you."

"No need to get upset." Dez kept his voice low to soothe the agitated man. "Alex just wanted me to clear this up before I took the cheque to the cops. They'll want to verify your story, of course. But the fact that Shannon called you and you mailed the cheque will make a difference."

"Why?" Parker snapped.

"Because of the circumstances. If you'd been in Vancouver and had personal contact with Shannon they'd want to know the details. The fact that there's been a lot of friction between you and Shannon and now she's been murdered would raise some questions."

"I didn't say I mailed the cheque," Parker muttered.

"So, you did see Shannon in Vancouver."

"I didn't say that either. But yeah. I saw her. So what?"

"I guess that depends on when you saw her and under what circumstances. You didn't, for instance, see her last Wednesday? That would be the day she disappeared?"

"No, I didn't." Parker doubled-down on the scowl and fixed Dez with a glare that was approaching malevolence. I was there a couple weeks ago, and I haven't been back."

"Why don't you tell me what happened? I can't promise anything, but if you're telling the truth about not being in Vancouver when

Shannon was murdered, and I can verify that to the cops they'll likely be satisfied."

"You think?"

"It's possible. Now about your meeting with Shannon. How did that come about?"

"Like I said, she called me and said she needed money."

"Was your wife aware of Shannon's call?"

"No. It's complicated. Shannon wasn't exactly the kind of girl my wife believed her to be."

"How's that?"

"To put it blunt, she was a hooker."

"And you gave her money professionally?"

"What the fuck are you implying?" Parker's face flushed an even deeper shade of red and he bunched his hands into fists.

"Calm down." Dez spread his arms and shook his head. "I wasn't implying anything. I was asking—same as the cops will when they hear your story. You claim Shannon sold sex as a profession. So logically I need to know, did you or did you not seek out her professional services?"

"Sounds like shit when you say it that way," Parker muttered. "Look. I admit the kid kind of got to me and I struggled with it a bit, but no, I did not see her in the course of her profession. Is that straight enough for you?"

"Perfectly. And the money you gave her?"

"She claimed she wanted to get out of the lifestyle. Said she'd gotten herself clean, she'd been smoking crack—the money was the first installment on tuition for hairdressing school. I told her if she enrolled and got herself a part time job, I'd give her the rest."

"Did you tell your wife about this arrangement?"

"No, I didn't. I knew Shannon might be stringing me. So I figured I'd wait until she enrolled in the program, then if she played straight and got a job I'd tell my wife."

Parker leaned forward and cleared his throat. "My wife was pretty broken up when Shannon took off for the city. I didn't want her to know what the girl had been up to in Vancouver. I figured if Shannon kept her word and started school then I'd surprise Val by taking her over there for a kind of reunion."

"Nice."

"You being sarcastic?"

"No. I mean it. That was a nice thing to do. I'm sure it'll mean a lot to Alex."

"Yeah, well, I'm no hero, but I'm not a monster either. I didn't want to see that kid throw herself away on the street. I got to get back to my game."

"Sure. Thanks for your help." Dez said, pushing back his chair and offering his hand. "I know Alex will appreciate your candor."

"You're not going to tell him what Shannon was doing are you?"

"Not if I don't have to. I'll simply tell him the cheque was a down payment on Shannon's tuition to hairdressing school and leave it at that."

I think she wanted to change her lifestyle."

"Did she give you any hints about why?"

"Nope."

Chapter Seven

"Have they arrested Lyle Miller?" Martine settled into a chair at Dez's kitchen table and accepted the cup of coffee he handed over.

"No but they're about to. Hanson called last night to tell me their seventy-two hours was up, and they've decided to hold him as a material witness."

"Are you still convinced they've got the wrong man?"

"I guess you never know about people," Dez dipped his head and the long black hair he normally kept tied in a leather thong fell forward over his shoulder, "but it still doesn't feel right."

"It makes me mad that Detective Hanson is so set on the killer being Native."

"I don't think he has much choice. As I said earlier, there's a lot of pressure for action on this case. Stanley Park is a major tourist attraction and we're right in the middle of the season. The city fathers would very much like to write this off as 'one Indian killing another' and close the books. I could tell when I talked to him earlier that he's not sold on Miller, he just doesn't have anyone else."

"What reason would Lyle have to kill Shannon? Didn't you say he believed she was nineteen and she went with him willingly?"

"Same old stuff. According to their theory, Miller had a fit of passion and Shannon changed her mind and turned him down. He lost control and killed her, then he staged that elaborate scene in the park to make it look like a ritual killing."

"That doesn't even make sense. From what you've found out so far, it's likely that Shannon was a prostitute, and if that's the case, those girls don't change their mind, they simply raise the price."

"You don't have to convince me. Like I said, Mark doesn't even believe his own theory. It's just a matter of trying to get the mayor off his back."

"Did you tell him what you found out from Shannon's foster dad?"

"Yes, and he asked me to keep digging. Besides I've been thinking over my conversation with Parker, and I have an idea."

Martine took a sip from her coffee and set the cup down on the table. "What?" She gave him one raised eyebrow.

"Remember Amy, over at Evergreen House?"

"The one who told you about Shannon's date with Lyle."

"That's right. According to Ed Parker, Shannon was worried about someone."

Martine frowned. "Worried. How?"

"She told Parker some guy was starting to creep her out."

"Do you think it was her boyfriend? He's a bit on the creepy side."

"Maybe, but that's not the impression I got from Amy."

"Maybe one of her Johns. If the prostitution story Parker told you is true."

"Could be, anyway, Parker said Shannon had someone watching her back in case anyone got weird."

"And you think Amy might be that someone."

Dez shifted his long legs out from under the table. "Maybe," he said, getting to his feet and picking up his coffee cup. "I'll just take the chill off this. Want more?"

Martine held up her cup. "Half is good."

Cups refilled, Dez settled back at the table. "When I talked to Amy, I sensed that she was holding back. After what Parker told me I'm betting it has something to do with whoever was creeping Shannon out."

Martine nodded. "If you're right, it must be someone Amy knows."

"How do you figure that?"

"Don't you remember being a kid? We had our own code for everything. These kids have codes. It's one of those things that seems complicated to adults but makes perfect sense to kids."

"My childhood might have lacked a bit," Dez admitted. "Let's just say I was a loner."

Martine's smile warmed Dez's heart. "According to their code, it would be all right for Amy to tell you about Lyle because he's a stranger. But if Shannon was having trouble with a boyfriend, that would come under a completely different set of rules."

"Sounds feasible. How about coming with me over to Evergreen House? If she has any secrets Amy's more likely to trust you than a guy she sees as cop-adjacent."

"Of course." Martine put down her cup and stood. "I'll run over to my place for a few minutes. I need to call the office and speak to my assistant."

* * *

Half an hour later, Dez pulled into the driveway of Evergreen House, switched off the ignition, and turned to Martine. "I can try." Martine hopped out of the Jeep and followed Dez up the front steps.

"Hello, Mrs. Lawrence." Martine stepped forward, so the woman could easily recognize her through the screen door. "It's nice to see you again. Although I wish it was under more pleasant circumstances.

"Hello, Ms. LaChance and Mr. Pallaton." The thin gray-haired woman established recognition and pushed open the door.

"Come in," she said. "Do you have word on Amy?"

Dez frowned. "What do you mean?"

"Oh. I thought maybe you'd heard something from your detective friend. Amy's been gone since yesterday afternoon. I called the police, but they said they couldn't do anything until twenty-four hours had passed."

"I'll give Hanson a call," Dez said, indicating that Martine should follow Mrs. Lawrence inside while he stayed out and used his cell phone.

"Did you find out anything?" Martine asked minutes later after she'd reassured Mrs. Lawrence that they'd do everything they could, then returned to join Dez in the jeep.

"He's got an APB out now." Dez merged the truck into traffic. "Hanson was mad as hell when I told him the report had been called in last night and nobody gave him the heads-up. But what can he do, it's just too bad nobody in missing persons made the connection to Evergreen House."

"Understandable though, when you consider how many runaways there are in a city this size."

"Damn bad timing," Dez cursed. "I get a daily report of kids who make the missing persons list, but Amy hasn't been gone long enough."

"I know how you feel." Martine's face registered the pain of her thoughts. "I hate saying this, but if my suspicions are correct and we're dealing with an actual psychopath, it's probably already too late for Amy."

Dez slapped his hand against the steering wheel in a moment of sudden and angry helplessness. "Do you think there's a chance she dropped out of sight on purpose?"

Martine shook her head. "I can't see it. Amy is one of those kids that lives on the fringe of other girls' lives. I think any involvement with whatever secret Shannon was keeping was collateral on Amy's part."

Dez pulled into the driveway behind the condo and stopped the truck. Then, with his hand on the door handle, he turned to Martine. "I hate it, but you're probably right."

Chapter Eight

Dez decided to pay a visit to the Java Hut to see if he could expand any on Martine's findings. Might as well make a clean sweep of it, he told himself, starting from the park and working his way up the length of Commercial Drive. His first stop, a small café, yielded little reward.

"Do you remember seeing this girl?" He took Shannon's picture out of his pocket and held it out to the Chinese woman behind the counter.

"Not see." She shook her head in a confident negative.

"Okay, thanks." Dez pocketed the picture. He continued down the street trying two more small coffee shops and a deli with no luck. Next stop up the street, Guido's Pasta House. He stepped inside and watched the middle-aged woman pull a towel out of her apron waistband and wipe down two tables in succession.

"You wouldn't happen to recognize this girl." Dez walked up beside her and held out Shannon's picture.

"What about her?" The tall bony woman flicked a strand of limp brown hair off her forehead and scowled at Dez.

"Her brother asked me to help him find out if anyone remembers seeing her last Wednesday," Dez said, sticking to the truth but holding back the real reason for his questions.

Recognition flashed in her eyes. She stared at Dez for several seconds before deciding. "I hope the brother has better sense than the sister."

"She was here?"

"Yes. She came in about four o'clock Tuesday afternoon. She was with one of those freaks with green hair."

Dez nodded encouragement. "What can you tell me about them?"

"Not much. We have our early dinner special on Wednesday and the crowd is pretty regular- young folks looking to save a little money."

"Had you ever seen either of these particular kids before?"

"No, they were strangers. That's what caught my attention—that and his green hair."

"But you're sure they were here between three and four."

"Positive. Now what's this really about?"

Dez made a split-second decision that the truth offered his best chance of getting her cooperation.

"Like I told you, I'm working for her brother. But what I haven't told you is that this girl— Shannon Perrault—" Dez held up the picture again, "was murdered Wednesday night."

"So. You're looking for the boy with green hair?"

"The boy is definitely of interest, but I'd also like to talk to anyone who might have spoken with Shannon- like yourself. Did you have occasion to speak with her, or did you overhear any conversation?

The waitress shook her head. "It's like I said, the boy did all the talking. They ordered, they ate, he paid, and they left. That's it."

"I'll need to turn this information over to Detective Hanson—he's the homicide officer handling the case—likely he'll be in touch. Do you mind telling me your name?"

"It's Nora, and I'll tell him same as I told you," she said, pulling the towel back out of her waistband. "Now if that's all, I've got tables waiting."

"Of course." Dez smiled and held out his hand for her perfunctory shake. "I appreciate your time."

In the next block, Dez approached the Java Hut. Stopping inside the door, he spotted a group of young people seated along the coffee bar.

"Nice place," he said, speaking to a tall lanky boy with carrot red hair.

"Thanks. We like it." The youth responded. "Care for coffee?"

"Sure, I'll have a tall latte."

While waiting for the coffee, Dez reached into his inside pocket and removed Shannon's picture. "Thanks," he said, when the boy handed over the coffee. "Would you mind taking a look at this picture?" He set the coffee cup beside him on the counter and held out the photo.

"What's she done?" The boy asked, suspicion clouding his eyes.

"Got herself killed." Dez swiveled his head to watch the reaction along the counter.

A skinny black-haired girl with pierced eyebrows approached Dez's end of the counter and peered over his shoulder. "That's Shannon." The girl whispered.

"What's your name?" Dez turned to face the girl.

"Lisa."

"Hi Lisa. Did you know Shannon?"

"Not really. I just recognize her from working on the project."

"Project?"

"We're part of a group working to save the rainforests and natural terrain in Clayoquot Sound. Shannon was one of our volunteers." The girl twisted several strands of long black hair between her fingers. Her eyes darted from Dez's face to his feet as she nervously answered his questions.

"Did you know Shannon's boyfriend?"

"Les. He's not really her boyfriend. They just hung around for a while. Anyway, they broke up last week."

Dez nodded and smiled to break the tension.

"I appreciate your help, Lisa. Shannon's brother asked me to see if I could find Les. Apparently, he doesn't know about Shannon and Alex wanted me to tell him—I'm sure he'd like to know."

Lisa's deep brown eyes, heavily outlined in black kohl, fixed on Dez's face as if memorizing his outline. "I'm sure Les didn't know anything about Shannon," she said. "He came in here yesterday morning, all excited. He said he'd come into some money and was taking off on a mission."

Dez tried to sustain a passive expression, but his eyebrows raised involuntarily. "Any idea what kind of a mission?"

Lisa shook her head. "He wouldn't say. Les liked to act mysterious. Most of us figured Mr. Guthrie had given him a special assignment."

"Mr. Guthrie?"

"Eugene Guthrie. He's our leader." Lisa's eyes lit up when she spoke. "If it wasn't for Mr. Guthrie, Vancouver Island's rainforest- or what's left of it- would already have been destroyed by the corporate pirates."

"Sounds like an impressive leader. I bet Mr. Guthrie could help me with my investigation. Do you happen to know where I might find him?"

Lisa frowned. "He's a lawyer. Maybe you could call his office. His number's in the phone book. I'll get it." She ran down the bar to a jumbled stack of books on the end, grabbed a ragged looking phone book and spread it open on the counter. "His office is downtown somewhere." She flipped through pages looking for Guthrie.

"Thanks. I appreciate that." Dez took a card out of his pocket. "My contact numbers are on this card. If you see Les or think of anything else, I'd appreciate a call."

"Okay." She turned the phone book around and pushed it over to Dez. "Here's the number." She pointed to the name Guthrie & Associates.

"You've been very helpful." Dez made a note of the address. "Thank you."

* * *

Outside, Dez flagged a taxi and requested the Pacific Centre on Georgia. Settling back on the seat, he considered his approach to the lawyer.

Probably won't see me without an appointment but at least I can scope out his office and schedule a time for later.

The Pacific Centre's soaring glass entrance opened into a lobby with access to several multi-storied office towers and an underground shopping center. The complex, in the center of Vancouver's financial district, consisted of ten separate sets of elevators, each with an electronic directory that identified the individual offices. Dez skimmed the alpha list of names, found Guthrie & Associates on the 12th floor of the south tower and proceeded to the first bank of elevators to the left. On the 12th floor, he followed a black and white tiled hallway until a double glass door displaying the name Guthrie & Associates in heavy black script identified his quarry.

"Hi, I'd like to see Eugene Guthrie," he said to the shapely redhead who peered at him through a pair of gold-rimmed glasses.

"Do you have an appointment?"

"No, and I suppose that's a cardinal sin." He flashed his best version of a good ol' boy grin.

Unaffected, the redhead shook her head.

"If you'll have a seat, I'll summon Mr. Guthrie's assistant. Perhaps she can arrange an appointment on short notice."

"Thank you." Dez strolled over to a row of chairs and took a seat. Moments later a plump brunette with a bright, round face trotted across the room.

"I understand you'd like to make an appointment with Mr. Guthrie." She stopped in front of Dez and smiled.

"Hello," Dez said, removing a card from his pocket and holding it out.

"It's a personal matter—concerning the death of a young woman working on one of the community service projects Mr. Guthrie is involved with. I realize this is an unorthodox call, but I represent the young woman's brother and I was hoping if you gave him my card and explained the situation, he might give me a few moments."

The woman studied the card and then nodded at Dez. "I can't promise," she said, "Mr. Guthrie is awfully busy, but I'll see what I can do."

"Thanks." Dez smiled his gratitude and sat down to wait.

Ten minutes later the assistant returned, motioned Dez to follow her down the hallway to a large corner office, where she opened the door and stepped aside for Dez to enter.

Behind the desk, a round faced man in his late forties or early fifties focused sharp brown eyes on Dez's face and waited for him to speak.

"Thank you for seeing me." Dez approached the desk and stuck out his hand.

"I'm pressed for time this morning." The man gave Dez a limp handshake. His high-pitched voice went well with his gray hair and close-cropped moustache.

"Yes sir, I appreciate that." Dez settled into one of the leather chairs facing Guthrie's over-sized desk. "I'm here on behalf of Alex Perrault. I believe you knew his sister?"

Dez kept his eyes trained on Guthrie's face. Sure enough, just for a second, something flashed, and then disappeared. Recognition? Guilt? Knowledge? Dez didn't know, but he damn sure intended to find out.

"I come across a lot of people in the course of my business and other activities. Is there some particular reason you believe I know this man's sister?"

"She's been working as a volunteer on an environmental project I understand you spearheaded. The Clayoquot Sound Group."

"There are a lot of young people working on my projects. I value them and admire their dedication, but naturally with so many, I don't know all their names."

"I understand. But Shannon—that's her name—might stand out for you because her name's been in the papers. She was murdered last week."

"That poor girl they found in the park. I didn't realize she was one of ours." Guthrie's mustache twitched, and his expression softened. "What can I do to help?"

That was more like it. At least this stiff-necked lawyer was finally showing some emotion. "Perhaps this picture will refresh your memory," Dez pulled out one of the snapshots and handed it across the desk.

"Yes. I remember now. Young girl—in fact I questioned her at our Tuesday meeting as to whether her parents knew where she was—most of our volunteers are older and I wanted to make certain she had parental approval."

Dez perked up. So, Shannon *had* attended the meeting Tuesday night. He needed to question those volunteers, find out if anyone knew where Shannon went after the meeting.

Dez held out his hand for the photo. "Do you have any objections to my attending one of your meetings and questioning the other volunteers?" He rose to his feet and placed Shannon's photo back in his pocket.

Guthrie studied Dez for several moments and then shrugged.

"The meetings are open, but as far as giving you permission to question anyone, I'm afraid that's not up to me. All those kids are volunteers, so any questioning you may choose to do will be with their consent."

"That's fair. I'm trying to help Alex find out what happened to his sister. I'm sure most of them will be sympathetic."

"I meant no offense," Guthrie came around his desk and offered his hand again. "I'm just being careful not to make commitments that aren't mine to make. We meet Tuesdays and Thursdays in the little house in back of the Britannia Recreation Center."

"Thanks," Dez accepted Guthrie's handshake, made less tentative by the revealing of Dez's motives.

Chapter Nine

The wind howled across the deserted beach, whirling sand into dirt devils and pushing them out over the churning waters. A boy and girl, college students from the University of British Columbia, walked side-by-side, hands clasped, enjoying the secluded stretch of Wreck Beach where 'clothing optional' remained the rule.

"I feel so free," the girl said, turning toward the boy and pressing her breasts against his chest.

"Wowza." He pulled her closer, his hands sliding down her back and gripping her butt cheeks.

"Not here," she whispered. "Someone might come along. Let's climb that hill. The weeds are thick up there, they'll hide us."

"Let's go." He grabbed her hand and started running, pulling her with him. Laughing and stumbling they reached the bank and scrambled into the undergrowth. When they entered a patch of cat tails the boy grabbed his girl around the waist and they tumbled to the ground mouths locked, arms and legs entwined, rolling together in a tangle of limbs until they lodged —girl atop boy—against an old log.

"That was awesome." Sarah laughed into the wind. Raising her head, she glanced over the fallen log. Abruptly her laughter turned into a horrified cry and she clung to the boy like a limpet. "Oh my God," she sobbed, hiding her face in his meagre chest.

"What's the matter?" The boy lifted himself into a sitting position. "I can't see anything." He strained his neck to peer over her shoulder and see behind the log. "Oh shit." He cursed, when a puff of wind blew the acid reek of decay into his face.

"She's dead," he whispered covering his mouth.

"How do you know?"

"Look at her face. No live person ever looked like that."

"Shouldn't we make sure?"

"Okay. But I'm telling you, she's dead." He eased tentatively over the log and pressed his fingers against her throat. "She's cold." He shuddered at the touch and yanked his hand away. "Like I said, she's dead. I volunteered at the hospital last summer. Once you get a whiff of rotting flesh, you never forget the smell."

"What should we do?"

"We're getting the hell out of here. If she was murdered the killer could still be around."

"Oh my God. What if he's watching us?"

"Be quiet. I'm calling 911 right now."

The boy spoke into the phone giving their location and describing the body.

"Come on." He pulled the girl to her feet. "There's a driveway a couple hundred yards up the beach. The cops are going to meet us there. Let's go." He grabbed the girl's hand and they ran back down to the beach and away from the horror in the reeds.

* * *

"You were right," Dez said, hanging up the phone and turning to Martine. "That was Hanson. The girl they found on Wreck Beach last night was Amy."

"Poor kid. She didn't deserve that. Nobody does, I guess."

"They found another medicine card. The Crow this time."

"Do you know what it means?"

"I think it's Law or Justice, something like that. Maybe the killer's trying to tell us he's above the law."

"Arrogant bastard. Is Lyle still in custody?"

"He's being released this morning. The cops found a witness that remembered seeing Lyle in the theatre Tuesday night. The witness swears that he sat two seats over from Lyle, who was alone, and neither of them left their seats during the film. The man remembered Lyle particularly because he was wearing a bear claw necklace. He asked about the necklace and Lyle told him it was a polar bear. The movie started at 8:30 and ended at 10:40. According to the

Medical Examiner Shannon died around nine so Lyle is no longer a suspect."

Martine shuddered. "I'm glad it wasn't Lyle, and I sure hope you're right about it being a white man. If the killer is Native our people are going to be the ones to suffer."

"The fact that Amy's a white girl will turn this into a witch hunt. Hanson's going to be under so much pressure to make an arrest that everyone who knew Shannon or Amy is going to be under some very serious scrutiny."

Chapter Ten

Martine and Dez shared a pizza while they brainstormed their next moves in the investigation. Things went great until Martine told Dez she intended on going to the Clayoquot sound meeting the next night. Without thinking, Dez blurted out that it wasn't safe, and he should go in her place. That, of course, had been stupid. Martine told him in no uncertain terms that just because he'd gotten into her pants, it didn't give him the right to go all macho protective on her, and in the future there would be no more shared pizza or anything else between them. She had stormed out the door and Dez had spent the night trying to figure out how he could get back in her good graces.

He decided it best to work from home the next day, and give Martine here own space in the office. He spent the morning working, getting some phone calls out of the way and updating his reports. For lunch, he threw a burrito into the microwave and ate while he finished his notes.

Finished with the paperwork, he headed down Commercial Drive, stopping at a flower shop for a bouquet, resplendent with color and fragrance. A gift shop on the same block sourced a tasteful ceramic vase and a card depicting a forlorn killer whale, in which he wrote his apologies for overstepping. He let himself into Martine's apartment and assembled the offering on the kitchen island.

Finished, Dez went home to wait.

He'd almost given up on getting a response in time to carry out the rest of his plan, when a sharp knock sounded on his door.

Wish me luck, he addressed the Ojibway medicine man hanging on his wall, then he opened the door and had to strain valiantly to smother his laughter.

Martine stood in the doorway with her hands on her hips and fire in her eyes.

"I suppose there's an explanation for someone entering my place when I wasn't home."

"I thought I smelled smoke." Dez kept his expression poker straight. "As your landlord it was my duty to make sure you were safe."

"And the flowers? I suppose you put them there to cover the smell." Martine couldn't keep the laughter out of her voice or the twinkle out of her eyes.

"Guilty." Dez wrapped her in his arms and pulled her into a crushing embrace. "I'm sorry. Can you forgive me for being a neanderthal?"

"Well…"

"Please. I can't stand having you mad at me. Besides, I've got a bribe."

"What?" Her eyes turned dark with suspicion."

Dez smiled and opened the door wide, so she could see the table beautifully set for two with a chafing dish in the middle. "Jambalaya."

"You're kidding. You made this." Martine approached the table and sniffed the air.

"A Creole friend taught me. Wait till you taste it with the bannock."

"Bannock too. Okay, she pulled out a chair. "You are forgiven."

They ate their fill and then discussed various aspects of the case. When Martine brought up the protest meeting, Dez cautiously suggested that they should have a code that either one of them could text very quickly if they were in trouble. Martine furrowed her brow in assessment but agreed that it was a good idea and they settled on Coyote as their SOS.

Chapter Eleven

Martine finished applying the last coat of dark red lipstick and stepped back to survey herself in the full-length mirror. Black hair hung to her waist, with a few wisps that had been twisted and sprayed into spikes at her temples. A thick layer of white pancake covered her face, and she'd lined her eyes with the kohl black favored by her new contemporaries. She needed to make sure she looked the same as she had when she stopped into the Java Hut. No use drawing attention to herself by leaving off the makeup.

Martine smoothed the purple miniskirt and checked the tops of the purple suede thigh highs that completed her new age costume. Satisfied, she grabbed her black suede bag and hustled out the door and down the steps to Commercial Drive.

The house behind Britannia opened into a large workroom and Diana greeted Martine as soon as she stepped through the door. Les wasn't there and Diana explained that he was on special assignment.

For the most part, the workers consisted of young college students, intent on making a difference to the environment. They were a lively group, excited about their cause and dedicated to protecting ecosystems which seemed to have no inherent ability to defend themselves from disastrous profiteering.

There were mailers to be stamped, posters to be fastened onto stakes for delivery to the neighborhood, and leaflets to be folded. Martine worked steadily for a couple of hours when she noticed several volunteers gathering their jackets.

Guthrie, who had not directly spoken to Martine throughout the course of the evening, but who she had noticed casting at least a dozen surreptitious glances up and down her body, appeared at her elbow.

"The others got here a couple of hours before you and I did." He leaned in close and Martine forced herself not to shudder.

"If you could finish up this last stack of mailers, it would be a great help." He rested his hand on her shoulder. "What do you say? Are you game to help me?"

Warning bells sounded in her head, but anxious to find out if he knew anything about Shannon, Martine forced them down to a muted hum.

"I guess I could stay for another hour to help you finish the mailers." Martine raised her voice to make certain the others heard her agree to stay behind with Guthrie.

"That's a good girl." He squeezed her shoulder and walked away.

For the next hour, Martine worked steadily, folding and sealing the mailers and then packing them in a box for delivery to the post office. Volunteers set their tasks aside and funneled out of the back room in ones and twos as the evening wore on.

Gradually she relaxed and forgot about being alone with Guthrie. Across the room, he worked on a box of posters, fastening them to stakes and stacking them into a crate.

Finally, finished with the last of the mailers, Martine, picked up her bag and walked over to say goodnight to Guthrie.

"Finished?" Guthrie closed the crate he'd been working on. "I certainly appreciate the work you've done today." He smiled and once again Martine controlled the urge to shudder.

"I can't let you go without at least offering some refreshments." His tone was apologetic, but his eyes were just *too wide*. The pupils were all but dancing in their protruding round ivory bowls. Mania? A nervous breakdown?

"Thank you, but I really don't need anything. I should be getting home." Martine held up her cell phone, typed 'Coyote' and pushed send. "My roommate's expecting me."

"Nonsense, I insist you at least have a glass of milk and a cookie. It'll only take a minute." Guthrie grabbed her arm and guided her towards a door at the back of the room. The energy in the room was wrong. Martine could feel it clear down to the oldest strands of her DNA- which were all but shouting at her to flee -but she had as yet no new information to show for the night's work besides, what, Guthrie gave off creepy vibes? She had to stick it out.

"I have everything we need right back here." He pushed the door inward and in the same instant gave Martine's arm a powerful yank, and dragged her through the open doorway.

A monstrous brass bed dominated the room. Desperate to get away she lunged at Guthrie, but he only spun her around and flung her down on the bed.

"No you don't my love." He pulled her arms behind her back and bound them with what felt like a leather belt.

"Help!" Martine screamed at the top of her lungs.

"We can't have that now, can we?" Guthrie crooned in a high-pitched singsong voice. He flipped her over and slapped a strip of duct tape across her mouth.

"There. Now we won't be disturbed."

Martine bucked against the mattress, using her legs to propel herself across the bed.

Guthrie pounced on top of her, flattening her beneath him and knocking the wind out of her lungs. His erection was apparent through the thin fabric of his slacks.

"Feisty little thing aren't we?" he spat, as he grabbed her legs and pried them apart. We'll have to fix that, but first, let's get these things off you." While Martine thrashed and bucked, Guthrie yanked at her skirt and panties until the seams gave, then mashed the balled fabric into his face and inhaled deep the musk of woman and fear. His eyes rolled languidly up and a loose, distant smile briefly replaced the mask of rage and frenzy.

Martine surged forward on the bed, flinging her bound arms, trying to smash them against Guthrie's skull.

He laughed and forced her back down on the mattress. Then he took a leather thong out of his pocket and tied one of her legs to the bottom bedpost.

Martine continued to thresh and buck, but to no avail. The more she struggled the more Guthrie laughed. He tied her other leg, then grabbed her arms and yanked them over her head.

Gripping both arms with one hand, he released the tie binding them together. Then, heedless of Martine's struggles to free herself, he grabbed her shirt, pulled it over her head, pulled it off one arm, then switched hands and pulled the shirt off her other arm and tossed it aside. Next, he tore free her bra and threw it after the shirt. Straddling her and pinning her arms, he removed first one and then the other arm from under his legs and tied her hands to the bedposts.

"There, now isn't that nice." He leaned back and clapped his hands together in front of him.

Martine kept her eyes on Guthrie as he rose from the bed, crossed the room and grabbed a chair.

"I want to tell you a story." He set the chair beside the bed and reached inside a drawer in the bedside table.

"I imagine you recognize these, you being an Indian?" He held up a deck of Medicine cards. Guthrie removed one card and laid it beside her on the bed. "The Snake," he said, then shook his head. "No. I've already used that one." He leered at Martine. "But, you know that don't you, my dear."

Martine watched his hands.

"I think this one has *your* name on it." He took out the fox and laid it beside the snake. "You didn't think I fell for your teenager routine, did you?"

He pulled his lips back in a creepy smile and stroked her belly.

"I know all about you and that pretend-a-cop boyfriend of yours." He moved his hand up to her breast. A loud buzzer sounded in the room and he pulled back his hand.

"I bet that's your boyfriend now." He walked towards the door. "Don't worry, this room is soundproofed." He gave her his evil smile and unlocked the door.

"I'll be back soon."

He stepped through the doorway and Martine heard his key turning in the lock.

* * *

As soon as Guthrie closed the door, Martine went to work on her bindings. Twisting and turning, now unconcerned about making any excess noise, she worked the buckskin until it stretched.

It's a good thing that idiot doesn't know buckskin has to be braided before it'll hold anything, she thought.

Freeing her hands, she pulled the bindings off her legs and grabbed her boots and what clothes she could from the floor where Guthrie had tossed them.

Got to get out of here fast.

She supposed it could be Dez, but what if something had come up and he was unable to respond to her message? She couldn't take the chance of waiting around to be rescued.

Raising the blind covering the window, she breathed a sigh of relief when she saw a sliding pane. She climbed onto the mattress to reach the latch and gave it a twist, then holding her breath she shoved on the frame of the window. The wood creaked, and she stopped to listen. No footsteps. Mentally praying that whoever pressed that buzzer would keep Guthrie occupied just a little bit longer, Martine opened the window wide enough to stick her head out, slide her body

115

around and drop down holding on by her fingertips. From what she could see the drop looked to be about three feet and she could only hope the ground wasn't strewn with broken bottles or used needles like too many alleys this close to Hastings street were.

Here goes nothing.

She let go and dropped landing in the soft mud of a flowerbed. She checked her arms and legs, no sprains and no broken bones. She'd been lucky. Standing and brushing off the mud as best she could, Martine ducked her head against the driving rain and ran as fast as her legs could carry her.

* * *

"I must be nuts letting you drag me away from my dinner table and out into this godforsaken rain in what is probably a wild goose chase." Mark Hanson grumbled as he and Dez sped across the city.

"I sure as hell hope you're right." Dez spoke through gritted teeth, "I didn't want her to go to that damn protest meeting, but she's one of those modern women who doesn't like to be told where she can go. I knew there wasn't any use trying to stop her, but at least I could get her to agree to a signal if she got into trouble."

"What kind of a signal?"

116

"That's what I've been trying to tell you." Dez held out his cell phone and Mark read the screen.

"It says Coyote, what's that supposed to mean?

"It means Martine's in trouble. That's the code."

"I suppose you know that this Guthrie is regarded as something of a philanthropist-not to mention the fact that he's a lawyer. I'm going to look like a damn fool going over there at this time of night questioning him about one of his volunteers."

"It's only eight o'clock, not exactly the middle of the night. Anyway, I'll take the heat, if it comes to that." Dez led the way up the steps of the small square house almost hidden behind the main Britannia buildings.

"I didn't even know there was a house back here." Hanson puffed his way up the steps.

"Guthrie's Clayoquot Sound Project has the right of use for five years and then it reverts to Britannia."

"Nice. Free land, free use, tax deduction, and a hero to the community."

"Won't be so nice if he knows what's happened to those girls and hasn't come forward."

"I'll do the knocking." Hanson stepped in front of Dez and rapped sharply on the door. The guard up front said he hadn't come out, so he's got to be in there." Several minutes passed with no answer, and Hanson pounded his fists against the door. "This is the police. Open-up or we'll have to bust the door down."

Silence for several long moments, then the sound of footsteps on hardwood, and finally the sound of a lock being turned, and a door chain removed.

"I hope you've got some damn good reasons for banging on my door this late at night." Guthrie opened the door fractionally and glared at Dez, then he turned to Hanson.

"I presume you have some identification?"

Mark pulled his badge out of his breast pocket and held it out for Guthrie to study.

"What can I do for you Detective?" Guthrie continued to stand in the doorway blocking their entrance.

"You can open the Goddamn door and let us in out of the rain, for starters. Mark's loud bark appeared to shake Guthrie who stepped back and pulled the door open without thought to asking for a warrant.

"I understood you had a group of young people here," Mark scanned the large room. "I don't see anyone. Do you know where they've gone?"

"Home, I expect, or wherever young people go when they finish work. Everyone left an hour ago. I was finishing some paperwork and then I'll be leaving myself."

"We're looking for one particular girl. She'd be new to your organization, about five feet five inches, slim build, long black hair, a Goth.”

“Hell, half the kids that come here are made up that way. There was a new girl here tonight. Can’t say I paid much attention. Guess she went with the rest.”

While Guthrie and Hanson talked, Dez paced the room. There was something bugging him – the energy was all wrong. He approached a closed door at the end of the room and tried the doorknob. It was locked.

“What’s in this room?”

Guthrie’s temper flared. “Now really detective, what business does this man have prowling around my quarters? I’ve been cooperative and answered your questions willingly, but that is my personal space, and without a warrant, well, I’m sure I don’t have to tell you the law.”

“Hey, I was just curious.” Dez raised his hands placatingly and stepped back from the door just as his nose caught a whiff of Opium perfume.

In one motion, Dez whirled clockwise away from the door, his right knee briefly raising, then pumping down and back as his upper body canted forward to drive the flat of his cowboy boot into the lock plate just below the door handle. The crash of the impact was loud in the empty space of the meeting hall. The door had buckled inward an inch, but it was compromised enough that Dez’s following left shoulder was enough to tear the remains of the deadbolt through what was left of the inner doorframe.

Guthrie screeched and raced after Dez.

"Whhhat the Hell?" Mark sputtered as he ran to the doorway and surveyed the scene in the bedroom. Dez was on the floor where he'd fallen when he crashed through the door and Guthrie was standing by the bed with a stupid look on his face.

"I smelled Martine's perfume." Dez stuck out his chin. "I'd know that smell anywhere. Where is she Guthrie? What have you done with her?"

"I have no idea what this lunatic is talking about." Guthrie addressed Mark, his barely suppressed panic bubbling just below the surface, but under control now that it was clear there was no bound victim in the bed "This is my private room. I stay here occasionally when I have late nights, or as was the case earlier this evening, when I have feminine companionship, I'm a single adult, and who I spend my time with and what I do with them is none of your business." He aimed the last remark at Dez, though his explanation all tumbled out together.

"As long as she's of legal age." Mark intercepted. "I don't suppose you'd like to give us the lady's name, so we can confirm what you've been telling us."

"No sir. I will not." Guthrie pressed his lips into a firm line. "The lady in question is certainly over the age of consent, and she's a reputable member of the community. She would not appreciate having her personal business bandied about because she happened to wear the same kind of perfume as some other woman, which is apparently what precipitated this nut case's attack on the sanctity of my private space."

Mark shrugged and looked at Dez. "Can't argue with that," he said. "Come on, let's go back to your place and see if she's made her way home."

Dez stood and brushed off his jeans. He was just about to follow Mark out of the room when his eye caught a glimpse of a multi-colored strap hanging down at the foot of the bed. It was obviously the strap to a woman's bag – exactly the color of the one Martine carried, and before either man realized what he was about, Dez grabbed the strap and yanked the bag out from under the covers.

"And just how do you explain Martine's purse hidden at the foot of your bed?" Dez waved the purse in Guthrie's face and Mark stepped forward to claim the bag.

"Is that right?" Mark fixed his eyes on Guthrie. Does this purse belong to the young woman who was here earlier this evening?

"I don't know." Guthrie said. "I found it when I was closing up the shop, and since it was late, and I was expecting company, I brought it back to my quarters and laid it on the bed. Subsequent events must have caused it to fall to the bottom where I didn't notice.

"I suppose you're saying you didn't look inside for identification?" Dez turned to Mark. "It's simple enough to tell if it's Martine's just by looking inside."

Mark nodded, then opened the purse and pulled out a wallet.

"That's hers." Dez said, and Mark lifted the flap and took out her driver's license.

"Is this her cell phone," he asked, pulling the phone out of the bag and holding it up.

"Yes, and she never goes anywhere without her cell."

Guthrie, who had been watching the two men, slammed his hand down on the bedside table. "Now look here. I didn't look inside the purse because I didn't have time. As I've already told you, I was expecting company. I only picked up the purse and brought it back here for safekeeping. In the morning I intended to call Craig, my volunteer coordinator, and let him look into getting the purse back to whichever one of the young ladies had left it behind."

Dez scowled. Bullshit, he muttered under his breath.

Mark put a hand on Dez's arm. "Hang on now. There's no evidence that things aren't exactly as he says. Let's go on over to your place and see if Martine's come home. She might have left her purse behind and by the time she realized she didn't have it with her, Guthrie had locked the front doors.

Dez glared at Guthrie but stepped towards the door. "Okay, let's go, but I still think you should lock this guy up until we find out for sure."

"You know I can't do that." Mark turned to Guthrie. "You weren't planning on leaving town, were you?"

"Certainly not, I have a law practice to run. Now, if if you gents would be so kind as to vacate these premises immediately, I might be willing to call all this an honest mistake and not press any serious charges for trespassing or vandalism or both."

Dez preceded Gus out the door and the two of them followed the path to the front of the house.

Why don't we swing by the precinct, so I can pick up a car, that way if Martine hasn't shown we can put out an alert, and if she's there, I can take care of getting myself back home?

"Thanks Mark. Sorry to have dragged you away from your dinner, but I don't believe Guthrie. He's too damn smug. I just wish you'd locked him up or at least brought him along until we confirmed his story."

"The fact that he's smug probably means he's not involved. I've been doing this for a lot of years and they don't generally rub your face in it unless they're sure of their ground. Besides, it's like he said, he's a reputable member of the community and a member of the Bar. I can't go arresting a private citizen and dragging him along without cause. Want me to lose my badge because you thought you smelled perfume and got a bad feeling?"

"No. I'm just worried." Dez pulled up in front of the police garage and Mark opened the passenger door.

"You're coming by the condo?"

"Sure, I'll check out a car and be right behind you."

* * *

Martine guessed she could stop at one of the businesses and use the phone to call Dez, but everything along the street was closed for the night, and besides, it would be her word against Guthrie's as to what happened earlier. He'd for sure claim she invented the whole thing.

Damn, why didn't I think to bring along a recorder.

The fact that he'd try to rape her still didn't prove Guthrie was a killer, but he'd showed her the medicine card and bragged about them. If she'd had her wits about her she'd have grabbed one out of the drawer. He'd get rid of them first thing, she knew that. She didn't have anything but her own experience to tell the police. Hopefully Dez would believe her. He hadn't liked the idea of her getting involved the way she did, and he just might decide she'd put herself in the position. Damn men, you never knew which way they were going to swing when it came to a woman and sex – half of them still believed that women were to blame for their

124

own rapes. She didn't think Dez was of that mind, but she'd been wrong before.

Winded and gasping for breath, she stopped in the dark alcove of a closed café, waited for traffic to clear, and dashed, practically naked, across Commercial Drive to the door of her building.

Shit, my keys are in my bag.

Terror had taken her out the window and across the four dark blocks of City back streets to the condo, but now that she was there, if Dez wasn't home, she couldn't get into her unit.

He's always forgetting to lock that side door into the garage, she muttered when she turned the corner into the alley and saw that both condos were dark.

Thank God. She breathed a sigh of relief when the door opened, and she slipped inside. The Jeep was gone so Dez was out somewhere. Maybe that had been him at Guthrie's.

What a mess. Martine approached on the workbench Dez kept inside the garage. Still soaked from running through the rain she looked around the room for something to keep her warm, still chilled she supposed from shock. Spotting an old canvas tarp hanging on one of the pegs beside the workbench, she took it down off the wall and gave it a shake, then wrapped it tightly about her shoulders, sneezing from the thrown-up dust. It was probably something Dez used to climb under the truck, but at the moment she didn't care if it was dirty, at least it would keep her warm. Gradually her shaking stopped, and warmth seeped back into her bones. The minutes dragged by as her blood was still suffused with the adrenaline of the escape and her mind raced. Had she been followed back? Did she lock the door behind her? She paced back to the side door and twisted the deadbolt home. That bit of security provided, she crouched into a protective ball beside the workbench, pulling the tarp tight around her and falling now into a fitful slumber as the sine wave of her arousal now dipped into the parasympathetic recovery of all post-shock victims.

*　*　*

Dez pulled into his driveway. There weren't any lights in either condo and his heart thudded against his chest.

Taking the steps two at a time, he pulled his keys out of his pocket and selected the one that opened Martine's door. He unlocked it, stepped inside and called her name in a loud voice. No one replied, and he called her name again. He listened for a minute and then walked towards the bedroom. Inside everything seemed in order. Martine, who was a bit of a neat freak, had made the bed before she left, and everything had been put away in its place.

Dez pulled the door shut, leaving it unlocked in case she came home, and he wasn't there to let her inside, then he checked his own apartment, more out of habit than anything else. Nothing was changed, and he headed downstairs to wait for Mark.

The next ten minutes dragged on so long that when Mark finally pulled into the driveway, Dez practically attacked the car.

"She not here," Dez blurted before Mark could open his mouth."

"I'm sorry," Mark leaned over and placed a hand on Dez's arm. "I'm afraid I've got more bad news.

"What?"

"Guthrie's in the wind."

"How the hell did that happen?"

He must have taken off the minute we left his place. I know you're wondering why I never put anyone on him, don't think I'm not kicking myself in the ass, but think about it: what did we have? A citizen with a perfectly logical story pitted against a distraught guy looking for his girlfriend."

"I think I deserve a little more consideration than a 'distraught guy'."

"No disrespect intended, I'm just trying to get you to see the picture from my point of view."

"Okay. I don't care." Dez slid into the passenger seat and closed the door. "Martine's still missing, we need to find her and fast. If Guthrie's got her, she's in real trouble."

"Something tells me she's going to be just fine." Mark grinned.

"Are you nuts, Guthrie's gone, Martine's missing and you're grinning like it's all a big joke."

"Nope not a joke," Mark pointed towards the garage, "just a mystery that's about to be solved."

Dez turned to follow Mark's pointing finger to the corner of the garage, where, wrapped in the old tarp Dez used to work on his Jeep, stood Martine."

"Oh my god," he grabbed the door handle, stumbled out of the car and nearly tripped over his own feet in his rush to get to her side.

"Where have you been?" He wrapped her and the tarp up in his arms and pressed his lips against the side of her face.

"I'll tell you, if you'll let me breathe," she answered, shaking her hair back from her face and looking up to see the relief in his eyes.

"Hi Mark," she said over Dez's shoulder. "I'm glad you're here. I have some things to tell you, but I don't have any proof, so I hope you're willing to listen with an open mind."

"Let's go upstairs," Dez said, taking her arm.

"You go ahead," Mark turned back to his car. "I need to call this in and get an update, and I'll be right with you."

Dez turned back to Martine. "Can you make it upstairs?"

"Of course, I'm fine, but I'd like to put some more clothes on."

"Sure. Your door is open. When I found your purse with your keys inside, I left it unlocked in case you showed up and I wasn't around."

"Thanks. I'll come over to your place once I dry off and get dressed."

Chapter Twelve

The fancy car turned off Commercial Drive into the alley beside the Java hut. The driver slouched in his seat and watched the entrance to the busy coffee house. Couples came and went over the next fifteen minutes, and finally a long-legged girl with blonde/orange hair came out the door and stood on the front steps. She lit a cigarette and stood there smoking mechanically and seemingly without much pleasure, looking up and down the sidewalk as if waiting for someone.

* * *

His legs ached and the muscles in his arms twitched, but he remained slouched low in the deep leather seat of the car, waiting and watching while his mind relived his last attempted conquest.

* * *

The girl crushed her cigarette beneath the heel of her boot, left the porch and turned into the alley. He sat up in the driver's seat and cranked the motor so it'd be nice and warm when she got inside. She came running. He turned on his lights, catching the flash of her leg as she ran. Dressed in a crop top and Daisy Dukes, the brown skin of her belly dimpled in the headlights. The sight made him drool and he wiped his mouth on his sleeve.

He leaned across the seat, opened the door and watched her slide over. He had to have her -- no matter the risk. He needed his release. "So glad you could make it," he flashed his teeth in a smile.

"We better get out of here." Her voice came in a sexy squeak.

"Don't worry." He laughed as she pressed her nose to the window, scanning for anyone who might have followed her outside. "You sure you're up for this?"

"Yes. But I don't have anything to wear. I did like you said and left everything in my room, just like I was coming back."

"Good girl. Don't worry about what to wear I'll buy you everything you need."

"Ohhh, this is so exciting. I've never flown before, especially not in a private jet."

"It'll be great, he rested his hand on her thigh and kneaded his fingers."

"Somebody might see." She moved slightly away.

"Nobody's going to see anything. We're going straight to the airstrip. We'll be out of here in an hour. You're not trying to back out on me, are you?"

"Oh no, I promise. She slid towards the edge of her seat and pressed her leg against his.

"Good. He pressed the accelerator and the powerful car shot forward. "Let's get to the airfield. We've got a plane to catch."

She giggled and nuzzled at his neck.

Her hot breath stoked his own internal fire and he caught his breath. Soon, he thought, very soon, he'd have his reward.

* * *

Martine turned the water on as hot as she could stand it and scrubbed until her skin tingled. I swear I can still feel his slimy hands, she toweled herself dry, and sprayed a thin spritz of Opium across her breasts.

In her bedroom, she put on fresh underwear and a pair of capris. Then she pulled a blue top over her head and slipped her feet into plush house sandals. I hope I'm not making a mistake, but right now I need him. She closed the door of her condo and knocked tentatively on Dez's.

"Hi there," he stood at the door smiling. "Feeling better?"

"Yes, thanks. I couldn't wait to scrub that creep's fingerprints off."

"I know. Don't worry. Thanks to you Mark's already located his car. He wants us to stand by, in case he needs your statement, but from the sounds of it they have things well in hand."

"How did they find him so fast?"

Your statement that you'd been held captive in that room gave Mark everything he needed to secure a warrant and search every premises associated with Guthrie. They found a map with Pitt Meadows Regional airport circled in red. Further checking revealed that Guthrie kept a small jet there, so it was a matter of putting two and two together. The cops spotted his car outside the Java Hut. He picked up that girl you described the other day."

"Diana?"

"Sounds like it. Although from all indications she went willingly."

"She would, but she doesn't have any idea why he's leaving town. She won't realize that she's in danger."

"Don't worry. Mark has her covered. They've set up a cordon around the airport. Once Guthrie's inside the trap, they'll never let him get on the plane. They've got the SWAT team there and a couple of first-class snipers. Their main priority is freeing Diana. One of the snipers will take Guthrie out if that's the only way."

"It probably sounds horrible, but after what he's done, I hope they do. He's a lawyer and he'll run circles around our 'justice' system if they arrest him and take this to court."

"I know it, but that's not our call. We've done all we can. Now what do you say to a glass of wine and some music to soothe the spirit.

"Are you trying to seduce me?" Martine looked up at him, eyes wide with an unreadable expression on her face.

"Not unless it's welcome."

"It just so happens that I did a lot of thinking while I was going through that ordeal and wondering if I'd ever get away from that monster. I know I've been adamant about keeping our relationships uncomplicated, but I'm beginning to think maybe I was hasty."

Dez's eyes lit up, and Martine smiled and held out her hands.

"Not so fast. I didn't say I was ready to toss all my reservations out the door, but right now a glass of wine and some very soft music sounds like just the prescription I need."

"Your wish is my command." Dez, his voice soft and throaty, picked up the wine bottle and glasses in one hand and reached for Martine's hand with the other.

"Why don't we sit here?" He led her into the living room, then slid his hand along her arm and guided her down beside him on the oversized sofa.

Gentle strains of flute music rose and fell in the quiet room. Dez's décor reflected his passion for nature. Brighter shades of red and gold in the rugs and wall hangings balanced the highly polished hardwood and the luxury of dark suede furniture enfolded guests like welcoming arms.

Martine leaned her head back and sighed. Her breath caught in her throat as she tried to speak. "This is nice."

"Good. Dez placed one of the wine glasses in her hand and lifted the other in a toast. "How about we drink to new beginnings?"

"Yes, I'd like that." Martine touched her glass to his, took a long drink and set her glass on the carved oak table and then she turned to face him.

"What now?" she asked, as Dez's hand, which had somehow remained on her arm after he'd joined her on the sofa, stroked upward from her wrist until his fingers reached the loose cap of her sleeve.

"It's up to you," he said, kneading her arm with his fingers.

Martine drew in a breath, let a little moan escape and turned herself full into Dez's arms.

Meeting her lips and drawing deep, he captured her tongue and wrapped in each other's arms they shared their deepest longings.

"Oh my God," Martine came up for air, and wrapped her arms around Dez's neck. "I need more," she whispered against his ear. "I need to erase every thought of that monster touching me. I might be using you; do you mind?"

Dez placed his finger under her chin and lifted her face. "Feel free to use me any time you want, and, if after today you decide you want things to go back to the way they were, then that's the way it'll be. Okay?"

Tears sprang to her eyes. "Thanks." She pulled a condom out of the pocket of her capris, handed it over to Dez to sheath himself while she slid her panties down her legs and kicked them aside.

Dez rolled her over on the sofa and mounted her in one swift motion, burying himself deep inside.

"Oh God, yes, please." Martine moaned and went with him.

Later, sated and exhausted, they curled together on the sofa. For a long time neither of them spoke, finally Dez propped himself on one elbow and looked down into her eyes. Damn I'm one lucky guy.

Chapter Thirteen

Phil pulled up in front of Wisdomkeeper's cabin and climbed the steps to the front door. "Sure would be nice if you'd bend your principles enough to get yourself a cell phone," he said, when Wisdomkeeper opened the door and motioned him inside.

"Why? If I had a phone, you'd never come out here, you'd just pick up the phone and yak at me until you told me all your business. This way you come out for a visit, sit down for a coffee." He set a cup in front of Phil and poured from an aluminum pot that had boiled down until it was black as coal tar.

"Okay, you got me there. This is important though- remember those four guys at the Remand Center who gave both of us bad vibes?"

"Of course. So what have they done?"

"Escaped. They all work in the laundry and somehow they managed to smash in one whole section of the wall. They made it look like a machine had gone into overdrive and thrown itself against the machine next to it and that took a line of them down and they all toppled against the back wall and

137

knocked a hole clean through the plaster. Took the plumbing out along that side, and made such a mess that the Warden had to phone Mission Prison to see if they could handle Emergency Transfers since you couldn't have all those men in there without any working plumbing."

"Makes sense but how did that give them an escape route?"

"Simple, everything was chaos, they had fireman in there and a whole plumbing team coming and going, so for about five minutes the doors from the back of the laundry to the outside were left open, and that's all it took. Apparently those four were all prepped and ready. They'd somehow acquired the same kind of coveralls the plumbers wear — probably took them out of a previous batch of laundry since the prison supplies their uniforms whenever they do work inside."

"Oh, I get it now. Pretty darn slick."

"Yep. They slipped right out the doors with the plumbers coming in and out, and it wasn't until nighttime check in that anyone realized they were gone. Gave them a head start of nearly five hours."

Wisdomkeeper shook his head. "They're probably clean out of the province by now."

Phil nodded. "It seems like that would be their best bet, but it doesn't bode well for anyone they come across along the way. I got a real stink of evil off that Calvin. Anytime someone has the hair on my arms standing up and stinging like that I know there's more than just ordinary meanness in the air."

"I got the same reaction. I pray nobody comes across that band, and I kind of hope they've taken off way up north. Let the Mounties track them down, or maybe with a little bit of luck they'll encounter a hungry polar bear. You might call it Mother Nature's way of handling a bad situation."

"I think maybe we should take a look when we invite the ancestors into our circle this afternoon?" Phil looked really concerned and Wisdomkeeper picked up on his friend's demeanor.

"Couldn't hurt. They may not know anything, but I don't see any harm in asking."

"Agreed. So let's go ahead and get our ceremonial program worked out and then once we've finished maybe we can go to your Sacred Ground and have our circle up there."

Wisdomkeeper nodded agreement and the two of them turned to working on their program for the upcoming Pow Wow.

* * *

Dez finished packing his case for the men's circle, while Martine watched him with a solemn look in her eyes.

"Is something wrong?" he asked, concern lacing his voice.

Martine laughed. "No, nothing like that. I guess I'm just in one of those sentimental moods. I love seeing you prepare for your

139

circle. What you do is so important to those men who attend. Maybe I'm just a little bit jealous of your time."

"Hey, I can cancel if you need me?"

"No way. I'd never ask you to do that. Ignore me, I'm just being female. Maybe it's coming up on my moon time."

Dez dropped the ribbons he was rolling up for his case and stepped over to take Martine in his arms. "You know I love you, don't you?"

"Yes, just as I love you. Now please get your stuff ready and I'll carry your drum case out to the jeep for you."

* * *

Outside, hidden from view behind the hedge that separated the garage from the townhouse, four men in plumbers' uniforms crouched and waited.

"Bout damn time he got his ass in gear and got the hell out of here," the one named Calvin muttered.

"Are you sure it's a good idea hangin around here?" A younger Metis youth named Nico asked, and another Metis youth named Jerrod joined in and nodded his head to support Nico's question.

"Seems to me we ought to boost ourselves a car and get the hell out of this city," the youngest member of the group, a Cree fellow named Kai, who didn't look to be much more than 15 or 16 years old, spoke up.

140

"And just what the fuck do you figure we'll do without a dime to our name? Hell we couldn't afford to fill up with enough gas to get to Abbotsford if we did lift one."

Nico and Jerrod nodded agreement. "Dez talked about his collection, and from what I heard, he's got enough stuff in there we'll be able to pawn it down on Hastings to at least get us out of the city and down the road a bit. Besides, the woman's not going with him. I know she's got her own vehicle because there's two of them parked in that garage, so it stands to reason she'll have a debit or credit card on her."

"So what are we going to do about her?" Jerrod asked.

"Hey she's just a woman. You figure she's too much for all four of us to handle?"

"No, I just wasn't interested in getting into any more trouble if we did happen to get caught."

Calvin spat on the ground. "Bullshit. You're whining like a baby. We'll take her down, gag her and tie her up in the bedroom, then we'll go through her purse, get what we need- including the keys to her vehicle- and after we take whatever we can use from his collection, we'll get the hell out and leave her tied up in the bedroom." Calvin laid out the game plan in a heavily enunciated mechanical chronology, as if to illustrate his frustration at having to spell-out a plan so obviously simple to people who were incapable of grasping its basic brilliance.

After all, hadn't he been able to find the condos?

"Now shut the hell up. They're finished loading the Jeep and he's getting ready to go. Once he pulls out of the driveway and down the road, I'll walk up behind her, stick this in her back" he brandished a long knife with a rawhide wrapped handle."

"We're not going to hurt her are we?" Kai's eyes widened in alarm.

"Of course not. I'm just going to use this to subdue her so we can get inside and then I'll take her into the bedroom and shove her down on the bed and leave her there while we get what we need and get the hell out of here. She won't even see our faces"

Kai nodded and settled back into silence while they waited for Dez and Martine to say their goodbyes with a long kiss, then she watched as Dez pulled out of the driveway and headed down the road.

Once he was out of sight Martine slowly climbed the steps to the front door. She looked deep in thought as she reached for the doorknob, and as she did so an arm came around her chest, binding both arms and holding her in a tight grip. Opening her mouth to scream another man stepped up and slapped a long strip of black tape over her mouth and stopped her from making a sound.

"Okay sweetheart," Calvin's arm went up to cover her breast and being careful to hide what he was doing from the other three, he squeezed and pressed his hard-on up against her backside. "You just hold still," he said taking her keys from her hand, "and let me get this door open then we'll all get inside and I'll take you back to the bedroom and settle you down so you can just rest comfortable until we get done with our business."

Martine's eyes were rolling wildly in their sockets with terror. She knew exactly what to expect once she got back into that bedroom, but his free hand was brandishing a cruel looking knife that appeared to have been fashioned with limited access to tools. These were dangerous men.

Oh great one, please let my spirit leave this place now, Martine petitioned her Creator, and with a deep sigh, she stopped struggling and let the monster push her into the condo.

In the living room, Calvin's three followers set to work going through Dez's collection and loading stuff into the bags they'd picked up from the plumbing truck.

"Good stuff in here," Nico said, "lots of gold and turquoise. We'll get some good coin for those rings, and look at the beaded belts he's got. Tourists eat them things up."

"Yep!" Jerrod held up a large soapstone carved replica of a polar bear fishing for salmon. "This stuff goes for hundreds of dollars at the Pow Wows, so we ought to at least get a couple bucks out of that bastard

Whitney who runs the crooked pawnshop down on Hastings."

"I wonder what's taking Calvin so long," Kai turned from loading a complete buckskin outfit into his bag. "Wonder what he'd think of this." He held up a leather bullwhip. "I think I'll go and ask him," he said, and when the others ignored his question, he set his bag down and headed for the bedroom.

* * *

After he'd dispatched the other three to the living room to fill their bags with loot, Calvin prodded Martine towards the bed with his crude shank. Once there he pushed her down on her back, then tore open the front of her blouse with his free hand while holding the knife's point directly in front of her eye.

"Ahh, it's been a long time since I've seen a pair of those," he rasped.

Martine hadn't bothered to put on a bra that morning, and didn't move to cover herself with the threat of the knife so immediate.

"I almost wish you weren't gagged," he said. "I'd like to hear you moan and scream while I'm getting off in you, but we can't be disturbing my young partners, now can we." Calvin positioned himself on top of Martine, struggling now to free his erect member from the coveralls while still holding the

144

knife in one of his hands and simultaneously trying to reef down on the waistband of Martine's leggings.

Martine remained motionless underneath him. Following her petition to the Creator, she had ceased to react to anything done to her. It was like her body remained, but her spirit had gone elsewhere; off to the Creators realm, where it was free to exist without pain or judgement. Her eyes still registered, however, and through Calvin's fumblings, her arm had come free from beneath the knee pinning it, and was seemingly disregarded - likely, she thought, because up to this point, she had not seemed to be a threat. While Calvin was now nearly hyperventilating and madly struggling to wrest the now tightly rolled leggings below Martine's thighs, she saw her chance and didn't hesitate.

The knife, held loosely in the hand that was trying to strip Martine's lower half, had inadvertently pointed laterally across his groin at Calvin's opposite thigh. Martine's free hand smashed against the rawhide butt of the shank and drove nearly its complete length into the hairy white flesh of Calvin's inner thigh.

"CUUUNNT!" he screamed, his eyes panic-wide and afire with hatred. One hand clamped around her wrist to stop the blade from being jammed in any deeper, and the other did the only thing it knew how to do. Years of incarceration, a violent and traumatic childhood, and a lifetime of poverty and desperation hadn't given Calvin much in the way of gifts, but they had made a survivor out of an otherwise unremarkable man. They had sharpened his instinct to strike back at anything causing him pain to be immediate and remorseless. In facilities like the Mission Institution, one's capacity for violent retribution was an asset that could make the difference between being accepted by an influential gang, or being raped to death in the shower. Calvin's brain had turned control over to hard instinct, and he watched through the red screen of his vision as his other hand jerked the jagged steel free from his thigh and plunged it, again and again, into the woman's chest.

Martine knew she had been killed. He felt the blade - it felt more like someone thumping their fist against her chest, but she knew. At the same moment she knew she had won. The shrieking animal atop her had been denied her body and denied his satisfaction, had been made to feel pain. She felt her body relax then, and her eyes smiled over the square of silver tape on her mouth. This was her triumph, and a warrior's death.

Kai burst into the room and spotted Calvin crouched between Martine's legs. Blood dripped from the knife he held and Martine's body lay motionless beneath him. "You fucking idiot!" Kai screamed. "You've killed her and now we're going to have everyone looking for us as murderers! We'll never get away! I should kill you myself!" Kai lifted the bullwhip in his hand and swung it wildly in the confined space of the hallway, but a whip was altogether useless in close quarters, and Calvin easily grabbed it with one hand and jerked toward him, while with the other he slashed out with the knife, fast as a snake, opening Kai's jugular and part of his windpipe. Kai backpedalled into the hallway, clutching at the source of the fountain of blood now painting the white drywall in crimson splashes.

The commotion had attracted the attention of the other two who now stood in the doorway to the adjacent living room, hardly able to believe the amount of blood still pouring from the neck of their comrade.

"Okay, you two want any of this?" Calvin brandished the glistening knife in their direction, his other hand clamped over his own bleeding thigh.

"Hey no man. That's your business. We're just stuffing our bags and getting the hell out of here."

"Okay then, let me get finished up in here and I'll meet you out there with the woman's keys, cash and credit cards." He gave them a final warning glare and turned back into the bedroom. A cursory examination of his wound told him that she'd missed the artery (the dumb bitch), and that he was in no immediate danger of bleeding to death.

Moments later he strode into the living room. "Let's get the hell out of here," he said. "I've cleaned up in there and from the looks of things the cops are gonna think Kai broke in here, raped the woman, and in the knife fight that ensued they both ended up dead. I've taken the tape off her mouth and pulled Kai's pants down. The situation ought to speak for itself."

"Hey, none of our business," Jerrod held up his hands. "You okay with that Nico?" he asked the other Metis youth, and Nico nodded his head vigorously in agreement.

"Okay let's move." Calvin picked up the bag that Kai had been filling, and the three of them left by the front door and headed into the garage.

Chapter Fourteen

Once they'd finished working out the details of their joint presentation, Phil and Wisdomkeeper picked up their pipes, and without a word they headed out the door and up the hill towards Wisdomkeeper's Sacred Grounds.

When they reached the Grounds they still hadn't spoken but it was clear from their actions that both were worried about something. They both felt the presence of a dark spirit that had settled like a cloud over them during the workup of their presentation. Something was wrong, they both felt it, but neither of them knew what. Walking slowly, a step by step climb up a slope that Phil wondered how much longer they could manage, they approached the Sacred Grounds and stopped at the entrance. The little clearing was, in a word, unremarkable. A small plateau on the hillside above Wisdomkeeper's cabin which provided a decent view, it could be said, but no ostentatious markers or totems to show that they were in a spiritually powerful place.

As host, Wisdomkeeper stepped forward and began speaking to the spirits waiting there, asking that he and Phil be granted permission to enter the Sacred Grounds. They walked forward several paces, sat down, removed their pipes and paid respect. Phil's pipe had been given to him by the Eagle Society, a Sundance community, and Wisdomkeeper's pipe was the one he carved while learning the lessons of the red road.

Phil started the ceremony by acknowledging White Buffalo, Calf Pipe Woman, and Orval Looking Horse, then he began a song which he continued while they loaded their pipes. They shared their pipes, passing them back and forth. After smoking for a time, sharing silent prayers, Phil began a song to each of the four directions. Wisdomkeeper joined in as they invited the grandfathers and grandmothers of the West, the North, the East, and finally the South-the going home direction.

As they raised their voices to invite the grandmothers and grandfathers of the south, an image of a young woman floated into their midst, and both of them recognized her as Martine. "Help me," she whispered her voice faint. She wore a gown of blood. "Come quickly. I don't have long."

"Did you get the feeling this is coming from Dez's place?" Wisdomkeeper laid down his pipe and turned to Phil. "We need to get there. She's in trouble."

"What about Dez?"

"It's Tuesday night. He's at his men's circle. There's no way to reach him. Let's go."

"Should we call the cops?"

"And tell them that we've had a vision of a woman covered in blood and ask them to go look in on her?"

"You've got a point." Phil joined Wisdomkeeper in cleaning out his pipe. They worked quickly to bury the ashes and pack the pipes back in their cases. "You can ride with me," Phil said, "and we'd best get on the road fast."

"I fear you're right."

Back at the cabin they stowed their pipes and Phil headed the jeep back down the dirt road and out onto the highway. It would take them at least an hour, but they'd get there as fast as traffic would allow.

* * *

Listening to the silence of the room, Martine opened her eyes and turned her head enough to see down the hall where Kai's body had fallen. One glance showed her the gaping wound in his throat and the red and white Jackson Pollock that had become the hallway. She closed her eyes and offered a silent prayer to the Creator for his spirit.

While she'd been unconscious blood had stopped pumping from her chest wounds, but as she gently tried easing herself up to more of a sitting position against the backboard, the blood started seeping from her chest again. Realizing the danger, she slowly pulled the sheet up to her chest and applied what pressure she could to as many

151

of the wounds as her balled-up sheet could cover. Quieting herself and slowing her breathing, Martine lay back and prepared to wait. If the Creator wills it, then someone in my circle has heard my message and they'll know something's wrong.

Phil drove as fast as he could get away with without risking being pulled over for a major fine. Fortunately, traffic wasn't as bad as it sometimes gets and that was probably due to them heading for the City during the lull before the afternoon rush hour traffic started. It still took them a full two hours and once Phil pulled onto Hastings Street.

Wisdomkeeper spoke up. "If you drop me at the Friendship Centre, I'll go in and talk to Dez."

"Sounds good." Phil agreed. "I'll head over there and let myself in - just this once you understand, extenuating circumstances and all that. Dez showed me where he leaves a spare, so I don't think he'd mind. I have my cell, so if things are as sideways as we think they might be, I'll dial 911."

"Good. I was just wondering about that."

Phil turned onto Hastings and pulled up to the curb directly in front of the Friendship Center, heedless of the 'Loading Zone' signage. "I'll drop you off here, and you can give me a call when you get Dez tracked-down and we'll make a plan from there.

"Okay. Give me a call as soon as you know Martine's condition. That's going to be the first thing that Dez wants to know. Wisdomkeeper got out of the jeep and waved a hand to let Phil know he was clear and turned on his heel for the carved front doors.

Inside the Friendship Centre Wisdomkeeper nodded to Annie at the desk and pointed towards the room where Dez held his circles. "I've got to give him a message," he said, and Annie smiled.

Inside the room about a dozen men sat around in a circle with Dez. When Wisdomkeeper walked into the room Dez saw him lift two hands to indicate he needed immediate attention.

"I've had something come up that needs my immediate attention," Dez said to the men. "I'm going to have to close the circle now. If everyone will join me in a prayer, thanking the Creator and the Ancestors, we'll close for today and finish up our discussions at next week's circle."

After the closing prayer everyone rose and respectfully cleared the room without dawdling, in order to leave Dez to take care of his business. The old man who had interceded was clearly distraught and it was not their place to question why.

"What is it?" he asked as he walked up to Wisdomkeeper.

"You've got to brace yourself brother. It's not good, I think."

"What?"

"Martine's in trouble. She might be bleeding, but we're not sure. We think she's at your house and Phil's gone to check.

Dez's face had set into a frozen mask. "Let's go." He surged down the hall with Wisdomkeeper right behind him.

"You need to prepare yourself," Wisdomkeeper said as he climbed into the Cherokee and fastened his seat belt.

"I know. How bad do you think she is?"

"I'm not sure. We were sharing the pipes when she walked into our circle and asked us for help. We figured there wasn't much point calling the cops and telling them we'd seen a vision of a woman covered in blood so we headed straight for town, still it took us two hours and I'm waiting on Phil to let me know how she's doing. He's gonna call for help if he gets there and it's as we think."

"But she was alive when you saw her."

"Yes. She was weak but she spoke clearly and she's a smart girl, not the type to panic. Let me borrow your cell phone and I'll try Phil, see if he's found anything."

Dez dug the phone out of his pocket and passed it across the cab. It rang as soon as it was in Wisdomkeeper's hand. He put it on speaker and said "Phil, I've got Dez here, we're on our way, what did you find?"

"We've got her." Phil said. "She's weak but she's conscious and the medics are working with her now."

"That is good news."

"Hey, Dez. Hang in there. She's lost a lot of blood, but she's a fighter and they're getting ready to transport her now. I'm following them and will probably get there right about the same time you do if you head for Vancouver General. I would have called sooner, but had to stay on the line with the 911 dispatcher.

"Okay, that's fine, Phil, but what the hell happened?"

"She was attacked. Stabbed a couple times. Looks like thieves, Dez - they took a bunch of your stuff."

"Stabbed! Jesus Christ. Are the cops there?" Dez's face darkened with his anger.

"They're here, askin a bunch of questions that I don't have the answers to, and Martine can't answer 'em either right now."

"Ok," said Dez, "we'll meet you at the hospital.

Wisdomkeeper put the phone back in his pocket and settled back in his seat. Dez focused on driving as fast as he could through the city traffic, and they rode in silence. Both men concentrated on getting to the hospital as fast as they could so they could see for themselves how Martine was making out.

Chapter Fifteen

Calvin kept Martine's car set to cruise at exactly 3 km over the speed limit. "We won't attract any attention, but we'll keep from pissing off any speedsters that get behind us." Leaving Hope behind and taking Highway 3 towards Keremeos, they kept an anxious eye on the gas tank.

"We'll need to ditch this one once we get into town," Calvin said, "hopefully we don't run outta gas before then. Too bad that bitch didn't have any cash in her wallet," Calvin muttered.

"There's cards," Jerrod reminded him.

"Sure, that's a smart move." Calvin snarled. "Her old man's probably home by now and the cops are all over that place. Once they discover her car is missing there'll be an APB out on it, and when they can't find her purse, they'll be in touch with her credit card company right off checking to see if her cards have been used."

Jerrod and Nico both nodded. "Good thing you're smart like that," Nico said. "I'd never have though about them tracking us down that way."

Calvin nodded and preened at bit at the recognition of his superior knowledge.

"We'll ditch this buggy in the bushes outside of town and then we'll make our way in and look for a likely target."

"How you going to figure that?" Jerrod wanted to know.

"Easy, an old couple. There's lots of them in this one-horse town - decrepit old bastards waiting to die." Calvin laughed. "Might be we can give them a hand with speeding that along."

"I don't think it would be smart to do any more killing though," Nico looked nervously at their leader.

"Hey, who the hell asked you to do any thinking," Calvin snapped. "I'll decide what we do with any hostages we have to take. *You* just keep your mouth shut and do what *I* tell you to do and *we'll* get along just fine."

Nico slumped back in the seat and turned his head to look out the window, clearly anxious about the predicament he found himself in

* * *

After abandoning the car on the outskirts of Keremeos, the three men slunk through bushes and ditches, being careful to keep out of sight from the highway until they were safely inside the town proper. Once there they strolled along acting like casual visitors until they came upon a Buy-Low Foods parking lot.

"Okay, you two stay out of sight here," Calvin motioned Jerrod and Nico towards a stand of brush in back of the trash bins.

"Watch for me because as soon as I get a car I'll pull up alongside this bin and you two be prepared to come on the run."

"Okay." Jerrod said and Nico nodded agreement.

Calvin watched until he spotted a young couple driving a pre-1990 Chevrolet, park their car and stroll hand in hand into the market. As fast as they disappeared out of sight he approached the car, opened the unlocked door, hopped inside, and set to work with a flat screwdriver and a pair of pliers that he'd purloined from the plumbers for just such an occasion. He pried the key tumbler free from the steering column, jumped the start wire to ground with the shaft of the screwdriver, then pulled up alongside the bins in the old blue Cavalier. As instructed, Jerrod and Nico piled into the back seat and Calvin sped out of the parking lot and pulled into a side street.

"How come you're stopping so close?" Nico asked.

"Because, smart ass. I spotted a couple of geezers walking towards their car. Watch and learn. Here they come now."

Calvin pulled out behind a white Toyota and applied his brakes to match the car's slow pace. The Toyota crawled through town at 35 KMH and Calvin kept two car lengths back. Finally when they cleared town limits at a bend in the road, the Toyota's signal flashed left and turned onto Maple Street. Keeping back Calvin waited in the turn lane until the Toyota pulled into the driveway of a neat little detached cottage.

"Perfect," he muttered as he executed the turn and pulled to the curb in front of a house that looked to be vacant. "Burg like this everybody will know everybody else, so best to pick a place no one's around in case we get noticed."

"Smart thinking." Jerrod agreed. "Want we should get out and wander up the street?"

"Yes, you do that. I'll hang out here until I'm sure they're both inside and then I'll go up and ring the doorbell. Gimme that woman's bag, we grabbed. I'll take it with me and when they answer the door I'll tell them I found it outside the market, figured it belonged to them and followed them here to give it back. Of course, they'll tell me it's not hers and I'll ask if I can come in while they phone the market to see if anyone's reported a missing bag."

"You figure they'll fall for that?"

"Of course they will. They're old folks, taught to be polite to strangers and help people in trouble. That's us: people in trouble." Calvin threw back his head and let out a nasty sounding laugh. The other two grinned and nodded approval.

"Okay, get headed down the street and check things out. Make sure there's no cops cruising the neighborhood. Then come back and ditch this old car somewhere."

* * *

"Howdy Ma'am," Calvin smiled at the woman who opened the door and peered at him inquiringly.

"Can I help you?" she frowned at the woman's bag he held aloft.

"Yes'm, I found this bag on the ground outside the market, and seeing you and your husband leaving the parking lot, I figured this must be yours so I followed you so I could give it back."

"Oh no, that's not mine. I have my bag."

"Oh, sorry, I guess I guessed wrong! I bet someone is worried sick about losing it. Do you mind if I use your phone to call the market and see if anyone's reported it missing? I'm not from this area and I'm afraid my cell phone is out of service here."

"What's going on, Martha?" The man from the marketplace appeared in the screen behind the woman and frowned at Calvin.

"Oh, this gentleman found a bag at the market that he thought was mine and when he saw us leaving the parking lot he followed to give it back."

"Oh, no sorry that's not Martha's."

"He wants to use our phone to call the market as his cell doesn't work here."

"Okay, come in. You can use the house phone." The old man opened the screen door and they stepped back to let Calvin enter the house.

* * *

"I don't know about Calvin's idea of grabbing this old couple," Jerrod said to Nico after they'd disposed of the car they'd stolen at the supermarket.

"Nope," Nico shook his head in agreement. "If you want my take we oughta get the hell out of here before *we* end up getting nailed for *his* murders."

"Just what I was thinking. Let's get the hell out of here. We'll take to the bush headed back towards Abbotsford, so we don't run into Calvin out on the highway, and once we're clear we'll try'n hitch a ride to the interior."

With that decided, they took off at a lope into the bush headed back in the direction they'd entered town.

* * *

"Hey, that's two of them right there!" Phil pointed towards the two men hitchhiking on the other side of the highway.

"I see. Okay there's an overpass up ahead, I'll take that and swing around to their side of the road and pick them up." Wisdomkeeper slowed to make it across to the other side and then headed back to where they'd spotted the two men hitchhiking.

"Need a ride fellas?" Wisdomkeeper had pulled the SUV to the side of the road beside the two men and Phil rolled down his window and spoke.

"Yeah. Thanks for stopping. We're headed towards Abbotsford, you going that far?" Jerrod asked as he walked up the side of the vehicle. Reaching the passenger window, he peered inside, smiling in an effort to look as congenial as possible, and recognition swept across his face. "Ohh, uhm, you guys...."

"Yup, us guys." Phil said. "We volunteered to help with the search for you. Thought maybe we could keep some mixed-up kids from getting hurt. Can't say as we're sorry to miss that snake you were palling around with," remarked Wisdomkeeper, scanning the ditch where the boys came from and checking his rearview mirror.

"We don't want nothin to do with that guy," Jerrod responded. "He's fuckin *crazy*, you know?"

"We know," Phil answered. "Now jump in and we'll help you fellas all we can. You're in a heap of trouble right now, and I doubt either of you would make it more than a week or two on the run. Plus, it just makes you look that much more guilty."

"We didn't stab that woman!" Nico volunteered from over Jerrod's shoulder.

"We know that too," Phil again replied. "We never figured you two for killers."

Chapter Sixteen

With the two young men settled into the back seat Phil turned to face them and offered each a bottle of water. "I'm going to make a telephone call to an RCMP officer I know, and I need you both to keep quiet while I talk."

"You ain't going to turn us in, are you?"

"I'm going to try and negotiate your surrender under terms that'll keep you from being implicated in the murders and hopefully mitigate some of the damage you're done by escaping in the first place."

"We didn't have no choice. If we'd have balked Calvin woulda killed us too."

"That's what I'm fixing to tell them. That and the fact that you're willing to surrender yourselves into custody and to testify to Calvin's crimes and assist them in locating and capturing him."

"Then he'll kill us once we get back inside."

"Nope. That's another part of the deal. I'll see that you get transferred up North to Prince George to serve your sentence. How'll that be?"

"Okay, I guess," Jerrod looked at Nico and the young man nodded. "I got family up that way. It'd be good to get as far as possible away from the mainland."

"Okay then. Now just sit back, drink your water and don't try to interrupt."

* * *

After an intense conversation that lasted the better part of the trip into Abbotsford, Phil hung up and stuck his cell phone back in his pocket.

"We'll go straight to the RCMP detatchment in Abbotsford," he told Wisdomkeeper. "Corporal Mitchell is giving them instructions to take these two into custody and hold them there until after we've captured Calvin. Then, as agreed, they'll appear before a judge to answer for escaping from custody, and Mitchell will have previously explained to the court the threat these two were under from Calvin, as well as their cooperation with the RCMP and their assistance in capturing a dangerous murderer. He'll also make certain that once the judge has remanded them into custody in Prince George as agreed, with hopefully no more than six months added onto their original sentences, they'll be transported up there."

"You both good with that?" Phil turned to the pair in the back seat, and both of them nodded eager agreement.

165

"Okay, we'll take you inside and turn you over, make certain Mitchell is notified of your surrender and then Wisdomkeeper and I are going to head back to Keremeos and see if we can't help locate Calvin."

"He's one mean dude," Nico shook his head.

"I'd stay the hell outta his way if I was you two," Jerrod echoed Nico's warning.

* * *

With the two men safely in custody, Phil's parting conversation with Mitchell had ended with the officer's assurance that once they'd interviewed Jerrod and Nico and gleaned as much information as they had to offer, he'd take them before a judge, get them processed, and as agreed, ship them north to Prince George to serve their sentences.

Chapter Seventeen

"You got any idea where we're headed once we get into Keremeos?" Wisdomkeeper asked.

"If I recall, Highway 3 runs right through the middle of town. We're about a mile out now." Phil rolled his window down and let his long hair blow in the wind. "We need a plan," he yelled over the roar of wind coming through the open window. "We've got to figure out what Calvin is up to before we go riding into town like a pair of cowboys."

Wisdomkeeper laughed. "You forgettin' we're the Indians?"

Phil joined him in the tension breaking laughter.

Wisdomkeeper slowed as they approached the outskirts and turned to Phil. "Where to now?"

Phil rolled his window back up to cut the sound. "I've heard they opened a Friendship Centre in what used to be the Anglican church over on 5th Street."

"Sounds good. Wasn't elder Glen Douglas from around here?

"Yep. I spent some fun summer weekends with Glen back in the old days.

He's moved on, but one thing about small villages like this one: everyone knows if there's a stranger in town. If Calvin's still with those old folks, and the police aren't savvy to that yet, he'll have had to cook up a damn good story to explain what he's doing hanging around their house."

"Probably claiming to be some kind of long lost relative."

"Maybe. That's 5th up ahead." Phil pointed as they approached an intersection. "Take a left. I seem to remember that church being a couple blocks off the main road."

"That look like the one you're talking about?" Wisdomkeeper pointed to an L shaped, white frame building with the typical mountain community's steeply peaked roof and a church's arched windows.

"Yep. That's the one. Timing's good to catch the morning coffee break, and I'm ready for one myself."

Wisdomkeeper pulled up to the curb, parked, and turned off the ignition. "Let's get in there and see if anyone knows anything about a stranger hanging around town."

"Morning," Phil spoke to the young woman sitting behind the reception desk. "Okay to go on in?" he nodded towards the slightly open door that allowed the smell of fresh brewed coffee to scent the air.

"Help yourselves. It's for everyone." She smiled a welcome.

The two men skirted reception and momentarily stood in the doorway.

"That's Lenard Raphael," Wisdomkeeper said, pointing to a medium sized indigenous man sitting at the head of a long table. Lenard had his long hair pulled back into a neat braid and around him sat several others who could have been brothers, or at least cousins, from the looks of them.

"Been a long time," Wisdomkeeper approached his friend with hand outstretched.

"John, I'd heard you'd gone on to the spirit world."

"A rumor, or maybe wishful thinking on someone's part," Wisdomkeeper laughed, and Lenard joined in.

"Grab yourselves a cup and join us. You remember Michael," Lenard nodded to the man beside him at the table, "and these are a few of my cousins."

"Good to meetcha. This is my friend Phil L'Hirondelle," said Lenard and lifted a hand in welcome, and the others responded with nods.

"I'll grab us a couple of cups," Phil said, and Wisdomkeeper took the seat next to Lenard that his brother kindly vacated and moved to a spot down the table.

"So where you been these past few years?" Lenard asked once Phil had handed a cup to Wisdomkeeper and taken a seat for himself towards the end of the table.

"Lower Mainland mostly. Got myself a cabin out in the woods over Hope way. Spend most of my time with my maliki friends. Seems I get along with four-legged's better than most two-leggeds."

Lenard nodded. "Probably a good choice. So, what brings you through this way?"

"Wondering if you've seen any strangers hanging around town lately."

"Funny you'd ask. We was just talking about this guy who showed up with an old couple lives over on the edge of town. Frank and Martha Thompson's their names. He was a schoolteacher and she was a nurse. They're good people."

Wisdomkeeper and Phil, both focused their attention on Lenard's statement.

"Fact is we're kind of looking for one or more men who don't seem to belong in these parts. This guy you're talking about, is he by chance a haole?"

"The one that's still around is, for sure. The other two that came in with him a few days ago were more'n likely Metis."

"So what's this white guy's story?" Phil spoke up and Lenard turned his attention to the man down the table who'd been introduced as Wisdomkeeper's friend."

"Best I can figure from what people who know the old folks been saying, he's supposed to be a nephew who hasn't been around for a long time." Lenard frowned and turned his attention back to Wisdomkeeper. "You know something about this guy we should hear about?"

"If it's who we think it might be, then this is one real bad dude," said Wisdomkeeper solemnly, "Got a lot of blood on his hands, and the sooner we get him away from the old people you're talking about, the better."

"That's no good." Lenard's attention shifted to the others sitting around the table. "Do any of you know this old couple well enough to drop by and see what's going on with them?" he asked the group.

Chapter Eighteen

It didn't take long for Wisdomkeeper and Phil to decide they'd be the ones to try to get into the Thompson's home, and fast. Didn't matter if they knew them, they were somewhat familiar with the escapees, so they'd take it from there. Best-case scenario, Calvin had moved on and the couple was still alive. Worst-case scenario … well, they'd get there and see what was going on for themselves before they started counting coffins. If they got there and it looked like Calvin was certainly there, they'd call in the cavalry and wait at the end of the driveway. Maybe they could deescalate the situation before it turned into an all-out blood bath. They felt with their experience and guidance they should be able to accomplish that, so they quickly prepared themselves for the intervention, should it become necessary.

"Do you think we'll even be able to get in the door?" Phil asked his friend.

"That's up to the Creator," was Wisdomkeeper's reply.

They quickly found the address they'd been provided with: a neat, whitewashed cottage with well-tended flowerbeds in the front yard. Everything looked fine on the outside, but they could only imagine what

Calvin might have put those poor people through.

Wisdomkeeper knocked. A tall slim man with a sparse white mustache and hair askew answered. He opened the door a crack and spoke through the screen. There was a purple bruise visible on one cheek as his eyes darted off to the side and back. He was clearly terrified.

"What do you want?" he asked in hushed tones.

"We'd like to come in," said Phil calmly, "and try to help you." *No way the horse cops will get here in time*, he thought.

Shaking his head no, the man tried to shut them out, but moving quickly, Wisdomkeeper managed to get his toe wedged into the crack before the door was closed in their face. Forcing the door as much as they dared, the two stepped into the room.

"You can't be here!" the man whispered hoarsely. "He'll kill us!"

Just then Calvin walked into the room holding a very frail, frightened woman in front of him. In his free hand he held a nasty-looking boning knife. "Gramps here is right," he sneered at Wisdomkeeper and Phil. "You've got no business pushing your way in here. You just signed this old lady's death warrant."

The Shamans didn't miss a beat. "It's all over, Calvin," said Wisdomkeeper. "Jerrod and Nico are already in custody."

Calvin tried to cover his surprise. "Yeah, well they always were stupid. You come all the way here just to tell me that? Thanks for the information, now get the hell out before I kill her, and don't think for a second I won't do it."

Phil spoke up. "You've still got time to end this thing before the police find you, Calvin. Give yourself up before you make matters worse."

Calvin's eyes burned with hatred. "And suppose you go on back and do whatever it is you like to do and leave me alone. As you can see, I'm busy."

Wisdomkeeper folded his arms. "Come on, Calvin. You need to let these people go. They don't deserve what you're doing to them. You can't just come into their home and threaten their lives like this."

Calvin laughed. "Ahhh, yes I can. I did, and I had a good thing going until you guys showed up. Always sticking your noses in, wanting peace. Well that's what I want too, and I got it, compliments of Grandpa and Grandma here. Grandma even fixed up my leg where that bitch stabbed me."

Phil reached out patiently to the killer. "Let these people go, Calvin. They haven't done anything to you."

Calvin's thin lips pulled into a wolfish smile that would chill anyone's blood. "It's not what they can do *to* me, it's what they can do *for* me, and I've found it quite comfortable here. Grandma is quite the cook."

The woman began to cry, her lips fluttering in what the two Shamans assumed was a prayer to her creator to be saved.

Calvin heard her and it ignited his hair-trigger temper. With a lightning move his arm left her shoulder and grabbed a handful of silky white curls in a punishing grip. She screamed pitifully.

Her husband lurched forward, as did Wisdomkeeper and Phil, but Calvin was quicker, the knife now at her throat. A tiny bead of blood trickled where the tip penetrated the soft pale skin.

Wisdomkeeper spoke firmly. "Calvin, you do not want to do this, you do not need to. Leave here, we won't try to stop you."

Calvin's eyes flashed fire. "You know it really pisses me off when someone calls me stupid! I'm five feet out that door and you'll have the RCMP on the line and give me up. Stop insulting me!"

Wisdomkeeper's gaze was even, his eyes never leaving Calvin's face. "Who's calling you stupid? Not us. Of course we're going to call the police, but you have our word we'll give you a head start, and then it's up to you whether or not you get caught. The other alternative is to end this right now. Stop running."

Phil added his voice. "We know you're tired of this whole thing, Calvin. No one likes being on the run, son. It's time to let these good people go. They have housed you and fed you, now it's time to put that knife down and be the man you probably always wanted to be. You're young, you can still turn everything around. I can't think that anyone would like living in this way, and I can see it in your eyes that you don't either."

Calvin's eyes shot toward the driveway and back. Wisdomkeeper and Phil simultaneously offered silent thanks that the killer had telegraphed this important information to them. He wanted to leave, and since it seemed unlikely he would ever surrender should it come to a fight, flight was the best option all way round. They had to get the knife away from this woman's throat. One tiny slip and her carotid artery would be severed. If that happened, there would be little chance to save her.

"Come on, Calvin, let the woman go," Phil urged him quietly. "Take their car and leave, man."

Calvin shifted his attention to the husband. "How much gas is in it?"

Renewed hope flared to life. "It's nearly full. Take it and go. You've seen where the keys are kept," he said, white-faced. "I beg you to leave my home, let my wife come to me."

Calvin's hostility was palpable. "Yeah, maybe I will take the car, but just maybe I'll finish my work here first. I'd be doing society a big favour, saving the taxpayers money.

You're old, and useless. The sight of you makes me sick."

Wisdomkeeper and Phil both saw fire leap into the old man's eyes. It would be a mistake to try to fight Calvin. There was no question as to who would win.

"Calvin!" Wisdomkeeper said sternly. "Take the car and get away from here, we promise to give you a head start."

Phil joined in. "Yes, one hour. We'll give you that much. You can go a long way in an hour."

Calvin cocked his head to the side, Phil now in his sights. "You know, I'm a real bad man with a knife. I've been in plenty of tilts, and I always come out on top. So one flick of my wrist and you can be next, mister Shaman. If I were you, I'd keep my mouth shut."

Calvin's attention swung back to Frank Thompson who was inching closer to his wife, maybe trying to surprise their captor. "You take one more step, old man, and wifey here gets cut real bad. Capiche?"

Thompson froze in his tracks. Calvin looked again at Wisdomkeeper and Phil. "Do I have your word on the hour's head start?"

They both nodded simultaneously. "You have our word. Just take the car and leave!"

The urge to leap forward and tackle Calvin was almost overwhelming as he shoved Martha Thompson forward and she fell heavily to the floor. Her husband was at her side in a heartbeat, Wisdomkeeper and Phil right beside him.

They heard the back door bang open and then the sound of the car engine. Since Wisdomkeeper and Phil had parked at the curb, Calvin quickly backed out of the driveway and hit the street on the run. Tires squealed as he took the corner almost on two wheels, and was gone.

The first call they made was for an ambulance for the elderly woman who was trembling violently. Her husband held her hand, explaining tearfully that she'd suffered a coronary only six months ago.

When they called the RCMP, they were able to furnish the make and model, colour and license plate of the Thompson automobile.

* * *

It took every bit of restraint Calvin possessed to slow his speed. Everybody that wore a police uniform would soon be looking for him. They probably already were, so he had to get rid of the Toyota, pronto. Fortunately, the old geezers he'd been staying with lived on the outskirts of town, so he grabbed the first road that would take him to the highway, and what should he come upon but the Buy-Low Foods supermarket. What better place to hide a car than a busy parking lot. He considered himself lucky to find a space in the middle of the pack. The store was a lot busier than the last time he was here. *Must be geezer cheque day*, he thought for his own amusement, although he felt about as much like laughing as he did having a pedicure. He had no interest in either.

He needed to lift another car, fool the cops at their own game. Then providence smiled on him when a young woman walked out of the store carrying two bags of groceries. He watched as she made her way to an old brown pick-up truck which he doubted had ever been shiny. It had more rust than paint. He hoped it ran all right though, because she was his ticket out of here.

She'd parked off to the side under the spreading branches of a hardwood tree, and he quickly slipped out of the Toyota. Unfolding his six foot plus frame, he sashayed over to where the woman was arranging the bags in the back of her truck.

"Hey, pretty lady," he walked up to her nonchalantly. "You wouldn't want to help out a poor ole country boy would you?"

She turned to face him and he realized he'd probably been the first to call her pretty in a while. Still, she had nice long hair and hazel eyes that might be considered attractive in some circumstances.

She smiled, and that did relieve her plain features a bit. "What's the trouble?" she asked him.

"Well, I need a ride. I got a job at a ranch up north and the truth is I'm flat broke until I get back to work. Could sure use your help."

She eyed him quizzically, still smiling. "Didn't I just see you get out of a car over there," she said, nodding in the direction of the main parking lot.

He smiled, and he *was* pretty. All the women said so. "You are right, I did get a drive with an old man, but this was as far as he was coming, and so I was planning to hitchhike from here." He tilted his head playfully. "Sure would be nice not to have to though."

She gave him a comical, long-suffering smile. "Oh all right, come on and jump in. Old Nellie here doesn't look like much, but she runs like a top." She stuck out her hand. "My name's Jo-Jo, by the way. What's yours?"

"Jason," he lied as he shook her hand. "Ahhh, I hope you're leaving right away 'cause I'm running late."

"No worries! I've got a lot of work to do yet today, and I can't spend it lollygagging around a grocery store. But, a body's got to eat, right? I noticed you're limping a little. Hurt yourself?"

"Yeah, got injured riding a bull. Trying to make some money."

She laughed "Riding bulls? You *are* brave. So how can you work if you're hurt?"

"Oh I can get around. Besides, I'm almost better. That was a month or so ago. Doc said it'd take a while for all of the soreness to work its way out. I've gotta work though, so what's a guy supposed to do?"

She turned to smile at him. "I like your spirit, Jason. What outfit are you heading to? Maybe I know it."

He shifted legs uncomfortably. "Can't think of the name of it right now."

She laughed and the shrill sound of it grated on his nerves. "How will you know when you get there then?"

"I'll know."

"Do you want to go and get your case? I assume you have one."

He smiled disarmingly. "You sure ask a lot of questions."

"I have an enquiring mind," she chuckled. "Seriously, grab your case and let's go."

"Don't have one. I'm travelling real light you might say," he said as he opened the truck's passenger door and climbed in.

Shrugging she slid behind the steering wheel and slammed the door shut. "If you knew where it is you're headed I'd be only too happy to take you part of the way there. I'd be willing to go a few extra miles to help you out."

"I thought you said you were busy."

"I am but I always try to put people first, and you're a people."

"That's right, I am."

"I'd have to stop for gas first though. My father's always teasing me that I run this thing on empty. I forget to gas up. It happens to me every time."

She sat waiting for vehicles to pass before pulling out onto the road.

"Hey, stop! You're going the wrong way."

She braked sharply. "Like I said, I'm low on gas so I'll have to go back that way to find a station," she explained, pointing in the direction he'd just come.

This couldn't happen! There could be roadblocks up by now. He leaned over and checked her fuel gage.

"You're all right. You're not on empty yet."

She looked at him, perplexed. "But I will be before I go very far and there's no gas pumps for a few miles in the other direction. No, I'll just...."

He pulled out the boning knife. "No, you'll go back the way you came. Now get moving, and don't try anything. Believe me, you won't like how it turns out if you do."

She blanched, but to her credit, she didn't scream.

* * *

As Wisdomkeeper and Phil headed home, after driving Frank Thompson to the hospital to be with his wife, they could see police cars everywhere.

Wisdomkeeper settled back in the passenger seat of Phil's jeep. "Do you think they'll get him before he kills again?"

Phil shrugged. "He's desperate, that's for sure. I'm just glad we were able to help the Thompsons. They'd both been abused, that much was obvious, but it could have been much worse. He could have killed them. It was good to see Mrs. Thompson already starting to improve once she was in the hands of the paramedics. Old roots are strong and they grow deep, but this will leave both of them with fear. They might have felt vulnerable before, but they probably hadn't invented a word yet for how they feel now.

Wisdomkeeper looked out at the passing scenery. "It makes you wonder what Calvin's life was like as a boy. Did he ever have a chance, or is the path he's on one of his own making. We will likely never know."

* * *

Jo-Jo kept the truck at an even speed under Calvin's watchful eye. "You do one thing to warn anyone, signal them, lay on the horn, whatever, and it will be the last thing you ever do," he told her. "I've killed before, I'll kill again. One more won't make any difference to me. I'll carve you up like a Christmas turkey."

She was still deathly pale despite her summer tan, but thankfully there were no tears. Weeping females drove him to distraction, and the ones that ran around screaming at every little thing really made him mad. He'd slit her throat in a second if she decided to do that. Grabbing an old straw cowboy hat on the seat beside him, he settled it low over his eyes.

183

"What are you going to do to me?" she asked, her voice shaking. "Are you going to rape me?"

"I wasn't planning to, but thanks for the idea. I might just treat myself at that."

He thought about the bitch back in the condo and how he'd been denied any satisfaction there. That still rankled him, stuck in his gut. He was due, and it didn't matter to him who paid up. Still, that one had been beautiful, but this one.... Of course, under the circumstances he couldn't be fussy, but he knew he didn't dare take the time. He half expected to come across a roadblock any second. In fact, they'd already seen two RCMP cruisers, but they were looking for the Toyota, not this rust bucket.

He glanced at the fuel gage, as if it would still be accurate in this old jalopy. They'd run out soon and they'd be stuck like sitting ducks on the side of the road.

He needed to get off into the bush. That was his only hope. There were plenty of lakes around here and that's just what he needed should they send the dog. His thought was that when they found the Toyota they'd be concentrating on Keremeos, and he'd be all the way up to Abbotsford, or maybe even back in Vancouver. He was sure he'd find a shortcut somehow, come across a farm or something. There were lots of them around these parts, and he'd get his hands on a vehicle. Or better yet, someone who could smuggle him out. Wouldn't that be sweet!

Get away right under the cops' noses. He was smarter than the law on any given god damn day.

He saw a break in the vegetation just up ahead. "Drive in there," he ordered her, showing her the knife again should she hesitate to obey him.

The old truck jostled and creaked in protest as it swung off onto the shoulder of the road and then onto the narrow trail leading into the bush.

"Okay, over there," he said. "Drive into that thicket and go as far as you can. I want this thing hidden from the air in case they decide to get ambitious and bring in a helicopter."

She did as she was told. When the truck could go no further, he grabbed the keys and, climbing out, hurled them a safe distance away.

"Now get out!" he ordered her, and this time he could see tears gathering in her eyes. She did so, and that's when she tried to break free and run. He easily chased her down, slamming her to the ground.

"Don't kill me," she begged him. "I tried to be nice to you. I tried to help you."

"And that's the only reason you're still sucking air, lady," he said, holding a fistful of her hair. "Now shut up and get your clothes off."

"Please...."

"Just get them off. You're big on top so your camo T-shirt'll fit me. You got a camo jacket? Something tells me you're a big-time camo fan."

"There's a jacket behind the seat, yes."

Pulling her to her feet he marched her back to the truck and held the knife in her face. "I said get undressed."

Sobbing she quickly divested herself of her jeans, T-shirt and underclothes, and he tied her hands securely behind her with her bra. He then ordered her back into the truck. He hoped she was the modest type because if she was naked, she was unlikely to run out of here and try to find help. He could just as easily kill her, but lucky for her he wasn't interested in a fight at the moment.

Quickly changing his top for hers and ditching the hat, he grabbed the jacket, found an old moth-eaten canvas bag in the truck and filled it with food from the grocery bags.

Jo-Jo crouched down over herself to cover her nudity, but he wasn't interested in that at the moment either as he set out at a trot into the bush, carrying the rest of her clothes. He'd dump them a ways in, not that she'd be looking for them he guessed. He looked up at the sky. He had to make the best of what daylight was left. By his reckoning he still had a few hours, and he could cover quite a distance before they found Jo-Jo and brought in the dog.

* * *

It was a sharp-eyed neighbour who spied the Thompson's car parked in the supermarket parking lot. He'd seen the drama unfold at their house, and someone squeal away in their Toyota. And now here he was pulling in next to it. He knew the car well with its slightly crumpled rear bumper where Frank Thompson had backed into the parking lot light standard. He called the RCMP.

Officers were at the market within minutes, and it took about five minutes more to meet the checkout clerk who'd glanced out the window and seen Jo-Jo Patterson, well known to store staff, talking to a tall dark-haired man. He'd gotten into her truck and left with her, heading toward home. Bingo!

* * *

It'd been years since Calvin had been in the bush, he thought to himself as he hurried deep into the woods. If the whole situation wasn't such a pain in the ass, he'd be enjoying himself right now. It'd been his grandpa who'd started taking him into the bush when he was just a little fart, and he'd taught him everything he knew. Take your time, never hurry was the first rule his grandpa had taught him, but he was already breaking that rule out of necessity. He had food with him though and he knew how to find water, and those things were in his favour. Finding a lake was his primary concern, and he'd waste no time getting into it when he did. Scent was hard to pick up in water. His grandfather had also taught him how to swim, and he did it well. So he'd keep

187

walking 'til he found a lake maybe and get some distance behind him, and then nature would be on his side. The cold water would also take some of the fire out of his earlier stab wound. It had really begun to throb with all this running.

An hour passed, or was it two? Maybe less.

He could hear a helicopter approaching and he ducked into a dense growth of trees, felt its vibration until it finally droned away. Reaching down he could feel the knife in his pocket. If they did spot him and send the dog, *he'd* end up sending the *dog* somewhere else. Hey, that was funny. He allowed himself a brief smirk, but now was no time for humour as he hurried along, his T-shirt soaked with sweat.

* * *

The young cougar caught sight of the man running through the bush and began to follow him. With soft footfalls the big cat kept his distance, the man racing headlong through the trees, tripping and sprawling clumsily onto the ground like a wounded animal. His senses rapier sharp, the cougar moved closer.

* * *

The helicopter made wide circles high above, brought in once it was determined Jo-Jo Patterson had not made it to the police roadblock a short distance away. Minutes later the truck was spotted about a quarter of a mile off an old road, and the missing woman was located. They now had a more precise search area, and Calvin was quickly spotted from the air. Rushing to set up a command centre, the Emergency Response Team assembled and began to kit up. The dog handler and his dog, Rako, were by now also on scene. The suspect had very kindly left his own T-shirt behind in the truck, and so armed with a good scent article for the dog, off the team went, weapons loaded and at the ready, and the frenzied Belgian Malinois positively straining against the long leash to run down the hot scent in the forest air.

* * *

Calvin hit the ground hard, a big man in a heavy face-first fall, but desperation shoved him to his feet and he began to run again, pell-mell, trying to watch behind as he ran. He didn't know what minute he'd hear the dog. He knew what that sounded like, felt like, to have a police canine set upon him. That's how they'd gotten him in the first place, or else he'd never been sent to jail. He quickly formulated a plan for this time around if he couldn't find a damned lake, and he'd enjoy jamming his knife into that mutt. It might get a bite in, but he was strong, and he'd get the upper hand fast enough. He'd slit its throat, if he didn't strangle the thing first.

He couldn't imagine they'd be on his trail this quickly. It was that bitch in the truck is what it was. He should have killed

189

her while he had the chance. That just goes to show, he grumbled to himself. You're nice to someone and they turn on you.

Winded, he took a moment to catch his breath.

* * *

The cougar watched the man intently, his large soft feet treading imperceptibly over forest floor bracken that would have snapped under the weight of a human's boot. But the cougar made no sound at all as it stalked its prey, steadily closing in on its quarry. It paused, watching, calculating as the man sat hunched, breathing heavily. One step closer, two, three, each one measured for a lightning-fast launching distance of two or three leaps. It was close enough now to spring onto the back of the man.

* * *

Calvin got up, making an effort to slow his breathing as he looked around warily. He remembered last time how the police were on him before he ever heard a sound. Were they watching him right now? He wheeled around in an untidy circle, stumbling as he did so. Why was he so unsteady on his feet? He was thirsty, that's what it was. Why hadn't that damned woman bought any water? And his leg was hurting like hell. Running had set the wound ablaze, and he could feel blood trickling down his leg. He looked. His pant leg was soaked with it.

* * *

190

The cougar was tensed for the strike, the crushed windpipe throat kill, but at the decision point, its keen ears picked up sounds. There was something in the wind. Smells of others like his current bloody prey, but more of them, and a dog. Danger. He would be denied his prize. Backing silently away, the young male disappeared soundlessly back into the underbrush.

* * *

Heaving the bag of food aside, along with the camo jacket, Calvin started ahead again at an even more frantic pace. There had to be a lake or pond around here somewhere, but all he could see was woods stretching out like an unrelenting maze ahead of him. He was heading to higher ground and the ascent winded him. He heard the helicopter again and dove into a swale off to his left and lay flattened, burrowing into the undergrowth as best he could. If they were in the air, they were also on the ground, and probably not far behind. He knew first-hand how well B.C's Southwest tactical unit was trained.

Spying a large boulder in a copse of trees he sprinted for it. This would be where he'd make his last stand if they were indeed closing in on him. Settle in and wait with his knife. Laying the weapon aside temporarily, he used both hands to dig into the soil, tearing away loose rocks and plant roots until his hands were sticky with blood. He

191

was on a slight rise and that would provide a good vantage point. He picked up the knife again. He was still breathing hard. He wished he hadn't left his own knife back at the condo with the bodies. Nevertheless, he'd make this work. It was as sharp as a razor. It was now a *him or them* moment, and while he might not be able to take them all, he'd get what he could. And then he heard the dog.

* * *

The team knew the killer's whereabouts had been identified, so did the dog. Calvin was just up ahead. Real close. They'd found his bag of food, the discarded camo jacket. They also saw the blood trail. Pain and desperation were making him careless. He was armed. He was dangerous. They saw the large protruding boulder in the copse of trees. Perfect hiding spot.

* * *

Calvin tried to quiet his breathing so he could hear properly. He was being stalked. He knew it, could feel it. Would they come at him from behind? Would it be a frontal assault? He raised his knife.

* * *

The copter left, having roughly ascertained the fugitive's whereabouts, and having just enough fuel to get back to base. The dog was now barking furiously, the handler holding him in check as the team, M4's aimed, moved soundlessly from cover to cover, surrounding the boulder outcropping, just out of sight. The whisper was so soft it might have been imagined to the ears of an untrained officer. "I have the suspect in my sights."

* * *

Calvin tried to remain calm, but he was already about a thousand miles past anything like that island of serenity. And then he heard the command: "Calvin! We've got you surrounded! Drop your weapon and come out with your hands up!"

Maddened by pain and fatigue, feeling the world crush in around him again, with knife aimed at his enemies in his extended fist, he surged forward with a roar in the direction of the dog. He'd kill it! He'd ram this seven-inch blade into that barking bastard, and anyone else he could get close enough to and make this all go away.

One weapon spit fire and lead, then the weapons to either side coughed three-shot bursts into the charging perp. The suspect was down. A menagerie of weeping holes in his chest and lifeless face.

193

Epilogue

In the cold light of dawn, three men sat in a circle. A smudge pot, filled with sage and sweet grass, natural tobacco and herbs, burned in a clay pot sending rings of dark colored smoke into the air.

"We are here to smoke the pipe and honor our sister Shannon." Phil raised his pipe, stem aloft, and offered the smoke to each of the four sacred directions.

"Great Spirit we have done your will, and worked with the law here on earth, and we give thanks to you for exposing the lies of the evil ones and uncovering their deceit.

The three of them shared the pipe in silence and when they had drawn and released the last of the smoke, Alex stood and spoke to the two Shaman.

"I don't know how to tell you how grateful I am to both of you for everything you've done for me and for Shannon."

"The journey to find the truth has been our gift as much as yours." Phil held out his hand to the young man.

Alex's eyes glistened as he took Phil's weathered hand.

"All my relations," Phil said.

"All is good here and in the Spirit world." Wisdomkeeper said, as he closed the lid of his case and stood.

The End

About the Author
Phil L'Hirondelle

Phil L'Hirondelle received his Cree Name from his grandmother Kokum Margaret L'Hirondelle.

Phil has worked with Indigenous people all his working life.

He is presently still working at 74 with Federal Corrections

doing ceremony and counselling for the over-represented Indigenous men & women. Phil has been a Sundancer for over 3 decades. He says the Sundance lasts 4 days but really it is the other 361 days that is the real Sundance.

As well as following his Indigenous culture, he also follows an Eastern teacher,

Master Dhyan Vimal where he also follows the teachings at the Dhyan Vimal Institute in Malaysia.

His goal is to bring the Indigenous teachings around the world.

I was taken from my mother at birth and adopted by a white family. I didn't find out until I was in my teens that I was from the north country of British Columbia, descended from the Sekani Nation (which means "mountain people") The Sekani are medicine healers, This book is dedicated from my heart to the many elders who shared their spiritual experiences and who embrace their cultures in the ways they live. My Indian name Sus' naqua ootsin' (the Wisdomkeeper) was given to me by a 100 year old lady who looked deep into my eyes and saw into my soul. My journey started on one of the darkest days of my life – when I finally decided to put on my red running shoes and follow the Red Road.

All My Relations…………

Sus' naqua ootsin'

BWL Publishing

bwlpublishing.ca

A Gift to the Reader

Wisdomkeeper has departed for the Spirit World but before he left he shared with BWL Publishing that he would like readers of **Ravens on the Red Road** to be gifted a copy of **Gifts from the Grandmothers**, which is added here as an Appendix.

WISDOMKEEPER
GIFTS FROM THE GRANDMOTHERS

Gifts from the Grandmothers

John Wisdomkeeper

Digital ISBNs
EPUB 9781772990379
Kindle 9781772990386
Amazon Print 9781772990393
BWL Print ISBN 978-0-2286-0583-6

BWL Publishing Inc.

*Books we love to write ...
Authors around the world.*

http://bwlpublishing.ca

the copyright owner and the above publisher
of this book.

Acknowledgement

Recipes shared by grandmothers from many cultures both Natives and non-Natives during my travels on the Red Road. Special recognition to Lillian Mack a very special Grandmother who has gone to the spirit world but who spent many hours updating these recipes with ingredients and methods that would work in modern kitchens.

Illustration by Mike Brodie

INDEX

Traditional Ceremonies: As a Metis person my experiences often differ from specific tribes and often contain teachings I have learned from many Native brothers during my travels.

Recipes from the Grandmothers: Recipes from grandmothers of many cultures shared with me by both native and non-native grandmothers.

Talking Stories: Stories told to Native children around the campfire to entertain and teach them moral lessons.

A Metis Traveler on the Red Road: My personal journal of experiences and people I met as I traveled the red road of sobriety.

Traditional Ceremonies
taught to me by Elders I met along my
travels

Smudging

Whenever our ancestors were suffering
from the "black clouds" of depression, they
used a smudge to cleanse themselves of
despair.

The smudge is a good way to prepare to
free ourselves from crippling emotions.
Find a calm, quiet place - go off alone into
the woods if possible.
Gather some sage and grasses, and prepare
your smudge in a seashell or other suitable,
fire-friendly container. Wash yourself
completely with the smoke, and make
certain to offer the smoke to each of the four
directions. Now lie back and very quietly
reflect upon the problems you are having.
Lift the problems off of your own shoulders
and send them out to each of the four
directions.

As you leave your place of smudging and
meditation, remind yourself that the
problems have been sent out to each of the
four directions and each solution will come
to you in its time.

The Vision Quest

In traditional times Native people used the Vision Quest as a way to reach inside of the dark places in their own spirits and come to terms with the anger and resentment that had accumulated there. The Vision Quest is a time of deep meditation and searching for direction. Alone, isolated from other people, we learn to spend time with nature, teaching us that we do not have to have human contact in order to keep us from being alone.

Mother Earth has many lessons to teach us, and it is only when we are alone and away from the distractions of modern life and other people that we can shut out the physical noise that surrounds us and open our inner ears to hear the lessons that Mother Earth has to teach us. A Medicine Man or Native Elder can instruct you in the procedure for preparing for a Vision Quest. A Vision Quest should only be attempted under the guidance of a Medicine Man or Native Elder. Now, in modern times, it is even more important that we begin to re-experience some of the traditional ways of dealing with extreme emotions.

The Pow-Wow

Ceremonial gatherings where Native people learned to get along with each other and to accept the different ways of other tribes were a part of traditional life.

In continuing these traditions, we hold the Pow-Wow. In our Pow-Wow celebrations, we gather together to dance and listen to drummers and singers, and share with each other the lessons of our ancestors.

It is during these celebrations that our youth learn about their culture and traditions and experience the feeling of oneness and community that comes from being with other Native youth, sharing experiences, respecting each other's cultural practices.

Native youth learn they are not alone, but that they are part of a distinct Nation deserving of respect and honor.

Just as it is important for Native youth to learn to be alone and to meditate and draw strength from Mother Earth, it is also important for them to socialize with other Native people and to hear the teachings of Native Elders so they can understand their own place in the Native community.

Sacred Pipe Ceremony

Smoking the Sacred Pipe has always been a part of our Native culture. Originally the pipe was smoked in friendship amongst the Native peoples to create the unity that was necessary for a strong Nation.

Our nation is scattered and fragmented within urban society, and it is important that Native youth find opportunities to participate in and be a part of those ceremonies that offer them the comfort and support of their cultural traditions.

Friendship Centers, Healing Circles and Native Elders in urban communities will know where and when a Pipe Ceremony is being held, and will gladly guide the young person to one of these ceremonies.

The Healing/Sharing Circle

In traditional times, members of Native tribes would gather into a Circle to discuss the needs of the tribe. Individuals with concerns would share them with the Circle, and the other members of the tribe would help the individual to work out their concerns.

In modern times, members of Native communities gather together into a Circle with other people from their community who are going through difficulties.

Each member of the Circle helps the other members deal with the problems they are experiencing.

It is understood by all that what is shared in the Circle stays in the Circle, so that everyone can feel secure that their problems and issues will not be discussed outside of the Circle.

Where to begin if you want to start your own Journey

Attend a sweat lodge ceremony

Participate in drumming or cultural dancing activities

Attend a pipe ceremony; visit a Medicine Man

Participate in a healing/sharing circle

Get involved in a cultural theatre project

Set up a schedule of creative enhancement activities

Share your feelings in a healing/sharing circle

Native counselors help youth gain pride in themselves

Smudging is a way of releasing negative emotions

A Vision Quest leads you to the root of your feelings

Native cultural group stress the unity of Native people

Knowing your cultural history brings respect

Learning cultural skills will give you confidence

Drumming is a powerful outlet for self-expression

FAMILY FEASTS

It is traditional for First Nations people to give thanks, and acknowledge our relations to the plants, animals, birds, and creatures from the water; to show respect for their giving their spirits in order for others to survive. Traditionally, elders say prayers to commemorate this sacrifice at a feast gathering. During these gatherings the people shared their recipes and often demonstrated the preparation and cooking of food. Elders would pass on ancient food gathering and preparation guides to the younger members of the tribe. Because of this tradition of passing on the wisdom of the tribe from generation to generation, First Nation's people became increasingly skilled in the art of drying and preparing foods, herbs, and berries with each passing generation. The Medicine men and women of the tribes were gifted healers trained by generations of ancestors in the art of using the gifts of Mother Earth to heal the people of their tribes.

NOTE: *Where possible recipes have been updated to include suggested modern ingredients and cooking methods suitable for today's home cooks. Special thanks to 95 year old Lillian Mack for her assistance in updating some of these recipes. Lillian Mack has now*

Soups and Stews

Buffalo Oven Stew

Two pounds of buffalo meat cut into 1 inch cubes. Note: Beef may be used if Buffalo is unavailable. Be sure to chop vegetables in uniform size so they will cook together and produce a flavourful well seasoned stew.

1 tbs. fat
1 large onion, chopped
1 1/2 tbs. salt
1 can stewed tomatoes
1 tsp. Pepper
4 carrots chopped
1/2 tsp. paprika
2 stalks of celery, chopped
1/4 cup flour
4 potatoes chopped

Fresh herbs such as basil, thyme, oregano may be added to enhance seasoning. For a spicier stew a tablespoon of salsa gives a nice zing. Brown buffalo cubes and onion in fat on high heat; reduce to simmer; mix flour, salt, pepper and paprika sprinkle over browned meat; stir and gradually add water to form gravy; Place mixture in casserole dish; add tomatoes, carrots, celery and potatoes and sufficient water to cover (leave room in the dish for the biscuit topping to be inside the rim of the dish) Place into baking dish, bake at 350 for 1 hour and 30 minutes; cover with biscuit topping and return to 425 oven for 15 minutes or until topping is golden brown.

NOTE: To get rid of the gamey taste of wild meat soak overnight in buttermilk, in the morning discard buttermilk and follow recipe.

Biscuit Topping

1 3/4 cups flour
4 tsp. Baking powder   1/4   cup shortening
1 egg
1/2 tsp. Salt   2/3 cup milk
Sift dry ingredients; cut in shortening to consistency of cornmeal; beat egg with milk; make a well in the center of dry ingredients; pour in milk mixture; stir until dough binds together; place on floured board; pat into circle, place on top of Buffalo Stew fit to edges of pan until snug; bake at 425 for 15 – 20 minutes or until top is lightly browned.

Basic Brown Stock

2 pounds beef or game (soup bones, shank, neck and ribs)
1 tbs. fat
2 quarts cold water
1 large onion, 1 carrot, 1 thin slice rutabaga

1 tbs. salt

3 whole cloves, 1 bay leaf

1/2 tsp. celery salt or celery leaves

1/4 tsp. thyme, savory or sweet marjoram

Brown meat in fat. Add cold water, cover and simmer for 1 1/2hours. Add vegetables and seasonings and cook for 1 hour. Stain through cheesecloth, cool and remove fat before using.

Squamish Corn Soup

1/2 lb. salt pork
2 big onions, sliced
3 cups diced boiled potatoes
2 cups boiling water
2 cups cooked corn, fresh or canned
4 cups hot milk
1/2 tsp. salt, pepper to taste

Dice pork into 1/2-inch chunks, add onion, cook slowly 5-10 minutes, stirring, until transparent but not browned. Add potatoes, corn, boiling water, hot milk. Season to taste, serve with garnish. To make a thicker chowder, make a roux of 2 Tbs butter and 2 of flour, frizzled, stir this into 1 cup of the milk, cook and stir until thickened.

Curried Squash Soup

3 acorn squash, cut lengthwise and seeded

2 carrots, chopped

1 onion chopped

1 tbs. vegetable oil

1 tbs. curry powder

1 can chicken broth

1/2 cup plain yogurt

pumpkin seeds for garnish

Fill large baking dish with 1 inch of water, arrange squash cut side down, cover and steam 10-12 minutes, until tender, let cool. Saute carrots and onion in oil 10 min., add curry powder, cook 1 min. longer. Scoop pulp from squash and add to carrot mixture, add chicken broth and 1 cup water, bring to boil, reduce heat and simmer 20 minutes, put soup in bowls and swirl yogurt into soup, garnish with pumpkin seeds.

Pea Soup With Wild Rice

Soak one pound of dried peas overnight.

Precook two cups of wild rice according to package directions.

½ pound of salt pork

Carrots, turnips, sweet potato

The next morning, add three cups of water and ½ pound of salt pork to large stew pot (or slow cooker). Add peas and bring to a boil then turn down to simmer. Chop root vegetables (about ¼ inch and all the same size for uniform cooking) Add vegetables to the stew pot and simmer covered for four hours.

Stir in cooked wild rice and add herbs like basil, oregano, thyme, sage. Simmer for another 15 minutes until herbs and rice are blended into soup.

Pheasant Soup

Pieces from several pheasants
1 teaspoon salt and pepper to taste
1 bay leaf
1/2 cup raw rice
1 cup raw carrots, sliced
1 small onion

Clean and wash bony pieces of pheasant well. Put in kettle with enough water to cover pieces add salt and bay leaf. Cook until meat is tender enough to fall from bones. Remove meat and bay leaf from broth. Discard bay leaf. Remove meat from bones in pieces as large as possible. Return meat and add a dash of pepper. Add uncooked rice and carrots. Cut onion in quarters and add. Simmer mixture for about one hour or until carrots and rice are tender and have soaked up most of the broth.

Roundhouse Pea Soup

1/2 cup dried split peas
 4 cups water
1 lb. Ham shank or 2 hocks
1 cup grated carrot
1 tsp. Salt
1 onion, minced
10 peppercorns, 1 bay leaf
1 cup milk
2 tbs. flour

Wash peas and soak overnight in water. Place ham shank or slow cooker, add peas and water in which they were soaked, add salt and seasonings, set to high, and allow to cook several hours. This updated version of pea soup allows for the use of a slow cooker. The recipe can also be made the traditional way by simmering 5 or 6 hours in a stew pot.

Moosejaw Chili

4   lbs.   course   ground   lean
beef/venison/moose
2 cloves garlic, minced
8 tbs. chili powder
8 tbs flour
4 tsp. salt
2 tbs. cumin
1/2 cup beef suet (may omit)
1/4 pound butter
2 cups onion, diced
2 quarts hot water
1 pint tomato puree
3 cups cooked kidney beans (optional)
Season the meat with garlic, chili powder, flour, salt and cumin, using your hands to work into meat. Heat suet and butter in heavy kettle and saute onions until soft but not brown. Stir in meat mixture and cook 20 minutes, stirring often. Add water and tomato puree. Simmer 2 hours, stirring often. If using cooked kidney beans stir in for the last 15 minutes.

Shuswap Corn Chowder

1/2 cup potatoes diced small
3 cups boiling water
2 tbs. onions chopped small
2 tbs. butter
1 cup cooked corn
½ cup celery chopped small
1/4 cup chopped tomatoes
1/8 tsp. pepper 1 cup milk (or ½ and ½)

Cook potatoes in boiling water until tender; do not strain; fry onion in fat until yellow and add to potatoes; add corn, seasoning and tomatoes; cook slowly 15 minutes; add milk and bring to boiling point (do not boil).

Klahowya Clam Chowder

Clams (2 or 3 dozen) or 1 tin
1/2 cup diced salt pork
1 shallot, finely chopped
1 onion, finely chopped
1 can chicken broth
2 cups diced potatoes
1/2 tsp. salt
1/4 tsp. coarse ground pepper
1 lg. can tomatoes
1/2 cup diced carrots
1/4 tsp. thyme

Wash clams to remove sand; place in a pot scarcely covered with water and steam for 20 minutes; strain and remove clams from shell; combine liquor with chicken broth and set aside; braise the vegetables lightly in large pot; add the clam broth and bring to a boil; chop clams coarsely and bring to a boil with tomatoes in a separate pot; add to the vegetables; add seasonings; simmer for ten minutes

Wild Vegetable Cream Soup

1/3 cup barley
2 wild onions, diced small
2 carrots diced small
2 potatoes diced small *always chop all vegetables the same size for uniform cooking
2 leaves wild cabbage or spinach, shredded
1 tbs. butter
1 tsp. salt
1/8 tsp. pepper
4 cups milk

Cook barley in boiling water until almost tender, 30 minutes. Add vegetables and enough additional water to keep from burning. Simmer until vegetables are tender. Heat milk, add barley-vegetable mixture, butter and seasonings. Simmer 5 minutes. Do not allow milk mixture to come to a boil.

Basic Bean Soup

1 pound dried white beans (soaked overnight in lightly salted water)
6 cups chicken broth
6 cups water
2 ½ cups sliced carrots
1 ½ cups chopped onion
1 ½ cups diced celery
1 can tomatoes (drained – reserve juice)
2 tbs. olive oil
salt and pepper to taste
½ tsp. hot-pepper sauce (if desired)

Add beans, broth and water to saucepan. Boil and reduce to simmer 1 hour. Skim foam off top, add vegetables –chopped small -- carrots, onions, celery, tomatoes, reserved juice and pepper. Return to boil, reduce and cook until beans are tender (approximately one hour) stir in olive oil, salt and hot pepper sauce. Serve.

Elk and Barley Soup

1 tbs. vegetable oil
1 pound chopped elk meat (may substitute beef) cut in ½ inch cubes
2/3 cup chopped onion
6 cups beef broth
2 cups diced carrots
½ cup barley
1 tsp. dried thyme
12 tsp. salt
1 pound fresh Kale (steamed and chopped) or 1 package frozen (may substitute spinach)
8 oz. Mushrooms (sliced)
Heat oil in skillet, add beef and onion and cook stirring occasionally, until meat is well browned. Add broth, carrots, barley, thyme and salt. Bring to a boil, reduce heat, cover and simmer 1 hour, add kale and mushrooms, return to a boil, reduce heat and cover. Simmer 5 to 10 minutes longer until vegetables are tender.Breads, Rolls and Preserves

Indian Fry Bread

2 cups flour
1 tsp. salt
2 tsp. baking powder
1/2 cup dried milk
1 tsp. sugar (optional)
1 cup warm water (or warm milk)

Mix ingredients and knead lightly, then pat out in 8" x 10" circles on floured board to ½ inch thick. Cut into pie-shaped wedges. Cut small slit in the center of each. Fry in hot fat until nicely browned. (Don't over-knead dough or bread will be tough) Garnish with a mixture of cinnamon and sugar – or jam or savory as desired

Pumpkin Loaves

3 cups flour
½ tsp. salt
½ tsp. baking powder
1 tsp. baking soda
1 tsp. ground cloves
1 tsp. ground cinnamon
1 tsp. ground nutmeg
2 cups sugar
3/4 cup butter or margarine (softened)
2 eggs
1 cup pumpkin

Sift flour and salt, add baking power, soda and spices; set aside; in large bowl of mixer beat sugar with butter until blended; add eggs, one at a time, beating well after each, continue beating until light and fluffy; beat in pumpkin at very low speed add flour mixture; mix until combined and smooth; turn into lightly greased loaf pans (2); bake 1 hour and 15 minutes or until tested done.

Sourdough Starter

2 cups warm water into container
1 pkg. Active yeast
1 level tbs. dried yeast
1 cup white flour
Mix ingredients to form smooth paste, cover loosely with lid, place container in warm place, leave for 24 hours. Sourdough starter can be kept in refrigerator for several weeks. Each time you use starter, pour off 1 cup of starter and set it aside as a starter for the next baking. Replenish by adding flour and warm water, nothing else. The mixture improves with time and once fermentation is under way, this cup of starter will be sufficient to sour the flour overnight.

White Sourdough Bread or Rolls

Put 1 cup of starter into mixing bowl
Add 2 1/2 cup of flour and stir lightly
Add 2 cup warm water
Mix thoroughly. Cover with plastic wrap.
Place in warm spot overnight (12 hours)
In the morning add:
1 cup water – warm
1 pkg. Yeast (1 tbs.)
1/2 tbsp. Sugar
2 tbs. butter
1 1/2tbs. sugar
2 tsp. Salt
4 cup white flour
1/4 tsp. Baking soda

Add yeast and sugar to warm water; still until yeast is broken down. Add to starter in your mixing bowl; liquid alternating with flour, stirring and adding until too stiff to mix with spoon. Turn out on floured board, kneading with hands, and adding more flour if needed to make soft dough. Briefly knead dough. Place kneaded dough in greased mixing bowl; cover with plastic wrap, and let rise until double in bulk. Knead briefly, divide dough into pieces to fill bread pans, fold into the shape of a loaf, place in warm greased pans, brush with melted butter, put in warm place, and let rise until double in bulk. Preheat oven to 425, bake loaves for 5 min. Reduce oven to 350 and bake for 20 to 25 min. Until bread is loose on sides of pans. For rolls follow above steps, but add 1 tbs. shortening and 1 tbs. sugar and shape into rolls and place on greased baking pan. Bake for 20 min. at 400 degrees

Rose hip Jam

2 cups rose hips, fully ripe (best after touched with frost)
4 cups boiling water
2 pounds sugar
¾ pound cooking apples

Wash hips add to boiling water, boil gently until soft. Mash, strain through a jelly bag, drip overnight. Measure juice, make up to 3 cups with water if necessary. Cook apples, rub through sieve. Mix juice and pulp, bring to a boil. Add sugar stir to dissolve, boil to jelly stage. Pour into sterilized jars and seal

Chokecherry Jelly

1 pound stoned chokecherries
to 3/4 pound sugar.
Stone cherries, mince
combine with sugar,

Let stand 2 to 3 hours, cook slowly, stirring frequently until thick. Pour into sterilized jelly glasses and seal.

Dandelion Sun Fritters

1 ½ cups whole wheat flour
2 tsp. baking powder
1 tsp. salt
1 tbs. melted butter or oil
1 egg (beaten)
1 tbs. sugar
½ cup flour
2 tbs. powdered milk
Pinch of salt
2 cups dandelion blossoms

Mix dry ingredients; add milk, egg and butter. Mix well, add blossoms which have been rinsed under cold water. Drop by spoonfuls onto greased griddle and fry until golden brown. Fold ingredients into flour mixture; bake 1 hour at 350. Test for doneness. Let sit 10 min. before removing from pan.

Campfire Bannock

5 cups flour (all purpose)
5 tsp baking powder
1 Tbs salt
1/2-3/4 cup shortening (lard)
Water

Mix all dry ingredients together. Cut in lard. Add water--enough that the dough holds together well, but not so much that the dough becomes sticky (if it sticks to your fingers-- add more flour). Once the dough is thoroughly mixed place on a greased baking sheet and pat down to about 1 inch in thickness. Bake at about 400-450F until the Bannock appears to be slightly brown. This recipe is also suitable for deep frying, frying, and pan cooking. To bake over a campfire. Divide the dough into palm sized balls. Shape each ball to about eight inches by rolling between hands. Wrap each dough length around a stick and bake over a bed of red-hot coals. Turn frequently to bake evenly.

Indian Harvest Bread

1 1/3 cup corn meal
2 quarts boiling water
2 tsp. salt
1 1/3 tsp. cinnamon
1 tsp. cloves
3 1/3 cups evaporated milk
1 cup molasses
2 cups sugar
1 cup raisins

Stir corn meal into boiling salted water and cook slowly for 10 minutes; stirring constantly; add other ingredients, mix well and cook in a double boiler 45 to 50 minutes.

Molasses Bread

2 cups Molasses
½ cup honey
2 cups wheat flour
1/2 cup white flour
1 tsp. cinnamon
1/2 tsp. salt
2 tsp. baking powder
2 eggs
1 cup oil

Combine dry ingredients and form a well in center. Add liquids and mix until smooth. Pour into loaf pan and bake in 350 oven for 30 minutes, or until toothpick inserted into center comes out clean.

Bush Biscuits

2 cups flour
1 tbs. baking powder
1 tsp. salt
1/3 cup shortening
¾ cup milk

Combine dry ingredients, cut in shortening with a fork or pastry cutter until crumbly. Add milk, mix with dry ingredients until they form a batter. Drop dough from a tablespoon onto a greased baking sheet. Bake in 450 oven for 10 to 12 minutes until lightly browned. To make smooth, rolled biscuits, increase flour until stiffer dough is formed, place dough on flour- covered surface and roll to approximately ½ inch thickness. Cut with large glass or biscuit cutter and bake as for drop biscuits.

Apple Bread

2 cups flour
¾ cup sugar
½ tsp. salt
1 pkg. dry yeast
½ cup milk
¼ cup butter
1 egg
½ cup pared and sliced apples
½ tsp. cinnamon
2 tbs. melted butter

Combine flour, ¼ cup of the sugar, salt and yeast in mixing bowl. Heat milk and butter over low heat, and add to flour mixture. Beat 2 minutes at medium speed. Add egg and ¼ cup flour. Beat 2 minutes at high speed. Stir in enough remaining flour to make a soft dough. Turn out on lightly floured board and knead until dough is smooth and elastic (about 5 minutes). Place in greased bowl, turning dough over to grease on all sides. Let rise until double in bulk (about 1 hour).

Punch down and cover. Let rest 10 minutes. Pat out dough to fill bottom of greased 9 inch square pan. Arrange apples on top of dough. Combine remaining 1/2 cup sugar and cinnamon and sprinkle over apples. Drizzle melted butter over the top. Cover and let rise in warm place until doubled (about 30 minutes). Bake 40 minutes in 350 oven.

Salads and Appetizers

Blueberry Salad

2 sm. pkgs. grape gelatin
2 cups boiling water
1 large can crushed pineapple (with juice)
1 pint blueberries
1 8oz pkg. cream cheese
½ pint sour cream
½ cup sugar
4 tsps. vanilla
chopped pecans

Dissolve gelatin in boiling water add pineapple with juice; add blueberries and chill until firm Topping: combine cream cheese, sour cream, sugar and vanilla, mix well; spread over firm gelatin; sprinkle with pecans. (*updated recipe to suit modern ingredients)

Cat n' Fiddle Salad

3 cups Fiddle Head Ferns Be Sure They
Are Not Unrolled (Open)
1 cup leeks
1cup Of cattail shoots (young
2 cups of lettuce
sunflower seeds to taste
½ cup Olive oil
wild garlic *may substitute regular garlic
Pick the fiddlehead when they are up to
6 inches in height and unopened wash these
and then drain. Chop leeks add to the
fiddlehead. Pick cattails early in the spring
also and peel first layer to get to the tender
shoots, the roots are also used as well wash
and chop and then drain. Cut up some
lettuce and add to the others. Add sunflower
seeds. Then add some oil and salt and
pepper, a little wild garlic is the best or
regular garlic.

Carrot Molded Salad

1 pkg. Lemon gelatin
1 cup boiling water
1 cup pineapple yogurt
1 cup grated carrots
1 tsp. lemon juice

Dissolve gelatin in boiling water and chill until slightly thickened. Fold in yogurt, carrots and lemon juice. Pour into mold and chill until firm. (*modernized to suit modern ingredients)

Bean and Egg Salad

1/2 cup mayonnaise
1 tbs. prepared mustard
1 medium onion
1 cup sliced celery
1 small cucumber
2 cans red kidney beans
4 hard boiled eggs
Seasoned salt to taste

Mix mayonnaise, mustard, onion, celery and cucumber. Fold in drained beans and eggs (cut in 1/3 chunks). Sprinkle with seasoning salt. Chill 2 to 3 hours.

Warm Cucumber Beet Salad

2 cucumbers, partially peeled and cut into ¼ inch slices
1 shallot, sliced
2 tbs. fresh or tsp. dried dill
½ tsp. sugar
¼ tsp. salt
2 tbs. vegetable oil
2 tbs. white wine vinegar
1 small head chicory
1 16 oz. can drained whole beets
Saute cucumber, shallot, dill, sugar and salt in oil for 3 minutes. Stir in vinegar and remove from heat. Place chicory on platter, arrange beets and cucumbers on platter. Pour warm dressing over salad.

Wild Cranberry Salad

2 cups ground fresh cranberrics
3/4 cup sugar
3 cups miniature marshmallows (or chopped whole ones)
1/4 tsp. salt
Mix well and refrigerate overnight
The next morning add
3 cups diced apples
1/2 cup walnuts
1/2 pint whipping cream (whipped until stiff) (or 2 cups of whipped topping) Fold into cranberry mixture and chill until ready to serve.

Cranberry Pineapple Salad

2 boxes cherry gelatin
2 cups boiling water
1 ½ cups sugar
1 bag (1 pound) fresh cranberries
1-16 oz. can crushed pineapple
3 apples, peeled
½ cup chopped pecans
Dissolve gelatin in hot water and add sugar. Grind cranberries and apples (chop fine in food processor). Add gelatin and remaining ingredients. Chill overnight.

Cabbage Slaw

¾ cup mayonnaise
2 tbs. soy sauce
2 tbs. vinegar
2 tsp. sugar
1 tsp. salt
1 cabbage shredded very fine
1-6 oz. can water chestnuts (drained and sliced)
1-6 oz. can bamboo shoots (drained and diced)
2 tbsp. chopped pimento
½ cup green onions chopped
Toss and Chill.

Jelled Beet Salad

1 pkg. Strawberry gelatin
1 pkg. Raspberry gelatin
1 pkg. Cherry gelatin
1 sm. can pineapple chunks
1 small can shredded beets
1 cup mayonnaise
½ cup chopped celery
¼ cup chopped onion

Dissolve gelatin with 3 cups water; add pineapple and beets. Chill until set. Combine mayonnaise, celery and onion and spread over chilled gelatin.

Jellied Cran-Apple Salad

2 cans whole berry cranberry sauce
2 cups boiling water
2 pkgs. Strawberry gelatin
2 tbs. lemon juice
½ tsp. salt
1 cup mayonnaise
2 cups diced apple
½ cup chopped walnuts

Melt cranberry sauce over medium heat. Drain, and mix cranberry liquid with water and gelatin, stir until dissolved. Add lemon juice and salt. Chill until mixture mounds on spoon. Add mayonnaise, beat until smooth, fold in cranberries, apple and nuts. Pour into 2 quart mold. Chill overnight.

Wild Ginger Carrot Salad

2 cups sliced cooked carrots
2 cups sliced celery
1 cup sugar
¼ cup finely diced preserved ginger
1 ½ cups white vinegar

Drain liquid from carrots (reserve liquid), combine carrots and celery in medium size bowl, stir sugar, ginger and vinegar into carrot liquid. Heat, stirring constantly to boiling. Cook rapidly about 15 minutes until medium syrup is formed. Pour syrup over carrot mixture, mix and chill overnight.

Rainbow Pea Bean Salad

1 can green beans
1 can wax beans
1 can red kidney beans
1 can chick peas
1 can lima beans

Recipe has been updated to use cans – 16 oz – home cooked vegetables and soaked and cooked dried beans and peas will produce a superior flavor

½ cup vegetable oil
¾ cup sugar
½ cup vinegar
Salt and pepper to taste

Drain beans and combine in medium bowl. Mix together oil, sugar, vinegar, salt and pepper; pour over beans and stir. Refrigerate several hours.

Strawberry wild Rice Salad

½ cup rice
3 cups water
1 pkg. Wild strawberry gelatin
½ cup sugar
1 small can crushed pineapple
Whipped topping
Cook rice in water until tender, drain, reserve water. Dissolve gelatin in 1/2 cup hot rice water. Add sugar, rice and pineapple. Refrigerate until partly set, add whipped cream or topping as desired. chill. Garnish with whole strawberries and serve.

Snappy Shrimp Salad

1 cup mayonnaise
1/4 cup Thousand Island dressing
1/4 cup chili sauce
1 tsp. prepared horseradish
1 tsp. Worcestershire sauce
1 1/2 tsp. salt
1/2 tsp. Tabasco sauce
1 lb. cooked, cleaned shrimp
Shredded lettuce
Combine ingredients, mix well and serve over the shredded lettuce.

Wahuwapa Balls

Ground Dried Corn Kernels
Dried Chokecherry or Saskatoons
Lard (or substitute water)
Grind dried flour corn kernels in a hand grinder. Grind dried Chokecherry or Saskatoons. Mix the corn and berries together at a ratio of 4 corn to 1 berry. Put lard in a frying pan and lightly brown the mixture.

Wild Meat Kabobs

2 lbs any wild game meat cut in cubes
2 tbs. Worcestershire sauce
¼ cup lime or lemon juice
1 tsp. onion powder
1 tsp. garlic powder
1 tsp. seasoning salt
1 bay leaf
¼ cup olive oil
Mix together all ingredients (except meat) pour over meat cubes and marinate overnight. Prepare bite size chunks of green/red peppers; tomato; mushrooms; onions; pineapple brush skewers with oil; alternate meat cubes with vegetable chunks on skewer; arrange on rack in oven and broil 3 to 5 min. turn and broil 2 to 3 min. Serve with hot pepper sauce or teriyaki.

Salmon Spread

2 envelops unflavored gelatin
½ cup water
1 can (16 oz) salmon
1 cup chopped onion
½ cup mayonnaise
½ cup sour cream
2 tbs. lemon juice
½ tsp. garlic salt
¼ tsp. dill weed
¼ tsp. pepper
4 sprigs parsley
Soften gelatin in water; dissolve over hot water; place remaining ingredients in blender; blend until smooth; mix in gelatin; pour into 5 cup mold; chill until firm; garnish with parsley, pimento and sliced green onion; serve with assorted crackers

Beef or Venison Jerky

8 lb Venison/beef roast
1 tbs. Salt
¼ tsp. Black pepper
1 tsp. White pepper
½ tsp. Red pepper
1 tsp.p. Meat tenderizer
2 tbs. Seasoned salt
2 tsp. Accent
1 tsp. Garlic powder
1 tbs. Kitchen bouquet
2 tbs. Morton tender quick
1/3 c Worcestershire sauce
1/3 c Soy sauce
1/3 c Barbecue sauce

Cut meat in thin slices. Combine salt, pepper, seasoning and meat tenderizers, add kitchen bouquet, Morton tender quick, Worcestershire sauce, soy sauce, barbecue sauce and liquid smoke. Marinate meat in sauce for 24 hours in a plastic freezer bag. Place meat directly on oven racks, line bottom of oven with foil and dry in oven for 6-8 hours on lowest setting.

Meat and Vegetable Dishes

Venison or Moose Cabbage Rolls

12 large cabbage leaves
1 tsp. olive oil
1 1/2 lb. Ground meat (may substitute ground beef)
4 tbs. grated onion
1/2 cup butter
1 1/2 cup cooked rice
2 tbs. chopped dill
3 cans tomato sauce
1 tbs. Worchestershire sauce
salt and pepper to taste

Brown meat and onion in butter, drain fat, mix in rice, dill, salt and pepper, Worchestershire. Core cabbage, steam until soft and easily removed, place mound of meat mixture in the center of each leaf, secure with a toothpick and place in lightly oiled baking dish, pour sauce over cabbage rolls, cover and bake 45 min. in 325 oven. Flavor is superior with wild meat, but recipe has been updated to accommodate modern ingredients. *NOTE: To get rid of the gamey taste of wild meat soak overnight in buttermilk, in the morning discard buttermilk and follow recipe.*

Herbed Rice for Wild Game Casserole

2 tbs. butter
1 green onion, chopped
¼ cup chopped parsley, ¼ tsp. Thyme, ¼ tsp. sage *
salt and pepper to taste
1 cup brown rice
2 ½ cups water
½ tsp. garlic powder
Saute green onion in butter until golden; add seasonings, salt and pepper, add rice and pour water over rice; boil until liquid is absorbed; transfer to covered baking dish and sprinkle with paprika. Bake 20 minutes.
*if available substitute fresh herbs.

Wild Game Casserole

1 onion chopped
6 oz. Extra sharp grated cheese
1 can cream of chicken soup, 1 can mushroom soup
2 cups cooked rice
¼ cup slivered and browned almonds
1 ½ lbs. ground meat (wild or beef)
1 can mushroom buttons and juice
1 cup shredded cabbage and green pepper
Brown onion, add meat, brown and drain grease, salt lightly, add remaining ingredients, and bake in casserole dish at 350 for 30 minutes. Serve with Herbed Rice

Creamed Cabbage

1 cup milk
3 cups shredded cabbage
½ cup half and half
3 tbs. butter
3 tbs. flour
salt and pepper to taste
Scald milk, add cabbage and cook 3 minutes; blend flour and half and half, add butter and slowly add to cabbage, cook 2 minutes longer, stirring constantly, add seasonings and serve.

Baked Game Hen

1 Game Hen
¼ cup flour
½ tsp. salt, 1/4 tsp. pepper
¼ tsp seasoning salt
Dash thyme and basil
Slice bacon and1 chicken heart
¼ cup melted butter
½ cup milk
Mix seasonings with flour, dredge game hen and bacon. Roll bacon around chicken heart, fasten with toothpick and insert in cavity of game hen. Brown hen in melted butter in skillet. Transfer to baking dish and bake 1 hour in 325 oven. Remove hen, sprinkle 2 tbs. flour in baking dish, place on burner at medium, mix flour with drippings, gradually stir in milk, bring to boil, stirring constantly until smooth for gravy.

Oven Fried Pork Chops

3 tbs. butter
1 egg beaten
2 tbs. milk
1 cup of corn meal stuffing (may use packaged)
4 pork chops

Melt butter in baking pan; mix egg and milk, dip pork chops in egg mixture; coat with stuffing mix, place chops in pan. Bake 20 minutes; turn and bake 10 to 15 minutes longer.

Spicy Beer Ribs

4 pounds spareribs
1 can beer
½ cup dark corn syrup
1/3 cup vegetable oil
½ cup chopped onion
1/3 cup mustard
1 to 2 tbs. chili powder
2 cloves garlic

Mix beer, corny syrup, onion, mustard, vegetable oil, chili powder and garlic; pour into plastic bag and add ribs to bag. Close bag and marinate ribs in mixture overnight. Remove ribs from marinade; place in shallow baking pan and bake in 350 oven 40 to 45 minutes, basting frequently with marinade. For excellent barbecued ribs, remove from oven and place on hot grill (6 inches) from heat until crisp brown on both sides.

Roast Tom Turkey

One good sized turkey
salt and pepper
2 tbs. melted butter or margarine
giblets
1 onion
1 celery stick
1 tsp. poultry seasoning (sage)
dried bread cubes (or box of stuffing mix)

Rinse turkey, pat dry and rub salt into neck and body cavities. Melt butter in small pan, chop or slice up giblets, add to melted butter with finely chopped onion and celery, brown lightly, add water and bring giblets to a boil, reduce heat and simmer 5 or 10 minutes. Combine poultry seasoning and bread cubes in large bowl, pour giblet mixture over bread and mix lightly to moisten stuffing. Chopped nuts, raisins, mushrooms, etc may be added to stuffing at this point. Lightly fill body cavities with stuffing, tie drumsticks to turkey with string, and secure neck cavity with turkey pin or toothpick. Place in 300 oven and bake 4 to 7 hours basting frequently with liquid from turkey baking. Baking time will depend on the size of the turkey. Test for doneness by gripping drumstick. When meat separates from bone when moved, turkey is done.

Chicken Fried Steak

1 to 2 pounds round steak
½ pound ground sausage
2 beaten eggs
2 tbs. milk
1 cup break crumbs
Salt and pepper to taste

Fry sausage, drain fat and set aside. Pound steak with tenderizing hammer, cut into pork chop sized chunks. Stir eggs into milk, dip chunks into mixture, then roll in bread crumbs, repeat egg/crumb process, then fry in reserved sausage fat until brown on both sides. Cover and cook over low heat for 45 minutes. Prepare milk gravy with fried sausage pieces and pour over chicken fried steak before serving. Serve with homemade biscuits.

Mashed squash

1 ½ cups squash
¼ tsp mace, ¼ tsp allspice, 1 tsp ground cardamom
1 tablespoon maple syrup
½ tsp salt
2 tsp melted butter

Cut squash in half, scrape out seeds and fiber. Chunk in 2" pieces steam for 30 minutes until tender (15 minutes if using electric steamer) Cool and skin, spoon into blender, add remaining ingredients and process till smooth. Makes a wonderful squash soup

Anasazi Dried Beans

Ham end or hock
2 Cups dry beans
Water to cover
1 large onion
Garlic – to taste
Salt And pepper

Soak beans overnight; drain water and add more to cover, cook beans till nearly done keeping them covered with water the whole time. Add ham and the coarsely chopped onion and garlic and continue cooking until all the meat falls off the ham bone.

Stir Fried Trout with Dandelion Greens

6 Handfuls Of Dandelion Greens
2 Trout
Grease (may use oil) to cover bottom of cast iron fry pan (or Wok)
3 Wild Onions – or green onions
Salt and Pepper, White Sage dash
1 Lemon

Cut and clean fish. Cut into long strips. Chop onion. Slice lemon into thin disks. Wash and chop dandelion leaves. Grease cast iron fry pan slightly with bacon grease. Medium heat Add onion 5-6 thin slices of lemon, salt, pepper, and a few pinches of white sage. Let cook about 3/4 of the way and then add the dandelion leaves. Cook until leaves are soft. Add salt, pepper, sage to taste.

Elk Tenderloin with Brandy Mustard Sauce

2 elk tenderloins, 8-10 oz each
4 slices bacon
½ cup sliced mushrooms
1 tbs. hot mustard
¼ cup onion, finely diced,
¼ cup bell pepper finely diced
½ cup brown gravy
1 ½ oz. Brandy
1 clove garlic
1 tsp. Thyme

Ground black pepper to taste Remove silverskin from tenderloins and rub meat with split garlic cloves. Sprinkle lightly with thyme and black pepper. Wrap bacon around tenderloin and use toothpick to secure. Place in hot cast iron frying pan and saute until bacon is cooked. Remove from pan and pour off excess grease. Place onion and bell pepper in pan for 30 seconds, add mushrooms and saute until tender. Add brandy to hot pan and flame. When flame dies, add brown gravy and mustard and stir until mixture is smooth. Pour mixture over tenderloins on warm platter.

NOTE: To get rid of the gamey taste of wild meat soak overnight in buttermilk, in the morning discard buttermilk and follow recipe.

Snappy Catfish

¼ teaspoon garlic powder
¾ cup yellow cornmeal
4 catfish fillets - or whole catfish
¼ 4 cup flour
2 teaspoons Salt
Vegetable Oil
1 teaspoon Cayenne Pepper
Combine cornmeal, flour, salt, cayenne and garlic powder. Coat catfish with mixture, shaking off excess. Add 1" layer of oil to a large skillet. Heat to 35~. Add catfish in single layer and fry until golden brown about 4-5 minutes; drain on paper towels.

Corny Turnip Casserole

1 large turnip
Salt to taste
1 cup corn (creamed) — may use canned corn
1 tbs. sugar
Pepper to taste
1/4 tsp. Nutmeg
1/2 cup milk
Butter
Cube and boil turnip in salted water; drain and mash; add rest of ingredients; place in greased baking dish; dot with butter; sprinkle nutmeg on top and bake 1/2 hour in moderate oven.

Indian Trail Beans

1 pkg. lima or pinto beans
2 cups cooked ham, cubed
½ small onion, chopped
2 stalk celery, chopped
1 small can tomatoes
1 green and 1 red peppers
1 tsp. baking soda
salt and pepper

Soak beans in water overnight; cook in large pan with plenty of water until well done (approx. 4 hours); add ham, celery, onion, green peppers, tomatoes and baking soda; season to taste with salt and pepper; cook slowly 45 min.

Hot Spiced Ribs

One or two racks of moose or beef ribs
3 tbs. flour and 1 tsp. salt and 2 tbs. fat
1 onion chopped
¼ cup cider vinegar, 2 tbs. brown sugar
2 tbs. Worcestershire sauce, dash Tabasco sauce
1 cup water, with 1/2 tsp. Dry mustard
¼ tsp. pepper and paprika mixed
½ cup diced celery

Combine flour, salt, pepper and paprika; rub into meat. Heat fat and sear the floured ribs. Lift into casserole. Add chopped onion to the fat in pan, cook and stir until golden brown; add all remaining ingredients and heat to near boiling. Pour mixture over ribs. Cover tightly and bake in 325 oven for about two hours

Golden Chicken Delight

Chicken pieces; skinned
3 eggs
1 cup milk
1/2 cup flour
1 cup bread crumbs
paprika,
salt and pepper

Line up three bowls. Whisk together egg and milk and place in first bowl. Add flour, salt, pepper and paprika to second bowl, Add bread crumbs to third bowl.

Dip chicken pieces in mixture bowl one; then dip in bowl two until coated with flour mixture. Dip back into bowl one and then dip into Bowl two, turning until coated with bread crumbs.

Fry in cast iron fry pan until golden brown on each side. Move to oven set at 350 degrees and bake 30 to 40 minutes until meat thermometer indicates 190F or 88C. If no meat thermometer is available remove thickest piece, cut into it with a knife and make sure there is no pink and chicken is fully cooked

Bear Meat Loaf

2 lb ground bear meat (may use ground beef – flavor will be slightly tamer)
1/2 cup milk
2 eggs
salt and pepper to taste
1/4 tsp. thyme
1/4 tsp. oregano
3/4 cup tomato sauce
1 cup onion, minced
1 1/2 tsp. dry mustard
1 cup bread crumbs
1/2 green pepper, finely chopped
1 small can of mushrooms or fresh mushrooms.

Mix ingredients & put in loaf pan. Bake at 350 until done (about an hour).

Sweet Potatoes Stuffed With Cranberries

1 ½ cups of cranberry sauce
3 tbs. butter
1/3 cup brown sugar
1 tsp. salt
½ cup chopped nuts

Bake potatoes until tender, peel skins and cut in half lengthwise. Scoop out insides and reserve. Stuff both halves, holding the potato back together with toothpicks. Mix sauce, nuts, sugar, butter, salt and pour over. bake at 350 uncovered until lightly browned, about 20-25 minutes

Stuffed Roast Pork Tenderloin

1 pound lean pork tenderloin
1 tablespoon all-purpose flour
3 tablespoons cornstarch
1 cup chopped onion
1/2 cup raw celery
1 clove garlic
1 bay leaf, crumbled
1 cup cooked wild rice
Trim all visible fat from pork. Split meat lengthwise, stopping about 1/2" from the edge. Open the split and flatten the meat out. Saute onions, garlic, celery and bay leaf Add 1 cup cooked wild rice and mix. Spread stuffing mixture inside the split meat. Fold meat back over itself. tie at 1" spaces with kitchen string. Bake at 350 degrees F, about an hour – (meat thermometer) 170 F or 77C.

Sweet Potato Harvest

1 can sweet potatoes *or 3 or 4 whole cooked
7 tbs. butter, melted
1 apple, cored and thin sliced
¼ cup brown sugar
1 tbs. flour
¼ tsp. Cardamom
1 tbs. butter
2 tbs. chopped pecans
Mash sweet potatoes until smooth, add melted butter; in small bowl mix cold butter, brown sugar, flour and cardamom, stir in pecans and sprinkle ½ over potatoes; cover with apple slices and sprinkle remaining mixture on apples; bake for 30-40 min. until apples are crisp/tender.

Salmon and Roast Garlic

Two medium heads garlic, broken into separate cloves, peeled
1/2 cup (about) olive oil
3 tablespoons unsalted butter
Eight 6- to 7-ounce salmon fillets
4 teaspoons fresh lemon juice
4 teaspoons chopped fresh rosemary
Preheat oven to 400°F.

Place garlic in small cast iron or ovenproof dish. Pour enough oil over to cover and cover with foil
Bake garlic until very tender, about 35 minutes.
Squeeze meat out of baked garlic into blender, add 1 tablespoon cooking oil and butter to processor; puree. Season with salt and pepper.
Increase oven heat to 450. Season salmon with salt and pepper and place on baking sheet. Drizzle each fillet with ½ teaspoon lemon juice, then spread 1 tablespoon garlic puree over each. (Can be made 1 day ahead; chill.) Bake salmon uncovered until just cooked through, about 15 minutes. Sprinkle with the fresh rosemary and serve.

Roast Duck with Apricots

One 4 ½ to 5 lb. Duck
¾ tsp. salt
¾ cup dried apricots, quartered
½ cup water
1 cup sliced celery
2 tbs. butter
4 cups ½ inch bread cubes
1 tbs. sugar
¼ tsp. leaf thyme
¼ tsp. nutmeg

Wash, drain and dry duck; sprinkle salt evenly over body and neck cavities. Prepare stuffing. Combine apricots and water in saucepan; bring to boil; cover and let stand 15 min. Saute celery in butter until tender; add bread cubes, sugar, thyme and nutmeg; add apricots with liquid and mix. Fill neck and body cavities loosely with stuffing; skewer neck skin to back; cover opening of body cavity with aluminum foil and tie legs together; place on rack in shallow roasting pan; bake in a 325 oven until drumstick meat is fork tender (2 ½ to 3 hours).

Whole Roasted Salmon

1 whole salmon, about 4 lbs., cleaned
Freshly ground pepper
1 medium onion, thinly sliced
1 lemon, thinly sliced
4-5 sprigs parsley, 1 tsp. dried thyme
1 Tbs. olive oil

Preheat oven to 400 degrees F. Rinse the salmon inside out and pat it dry. Sprinkle the inside of the salmon with salt and pepper, and stuff it with half of the onion, half of the lemon, and all of the parsley. Tear off a sheet of aluminum foil large enough to wrap the salmon. Place the salmon on the foil and sprinkle with salt, pepper, and thyme. Rub with olive oil. Scatter the remaining onion and lemon slices on top and seal foil tightly. Place on a cookie sheet and bake 40-45 minutes. Cool in the foil on a rack. Remove onion and lemon; skin if desired. Serve with pickled carrots

Pickled Carrots

1 pound carrots
1 tbs. mixed pickling spice
3 cups water, 1 cup cider vinegar
1 cup sugar, ½ tsp. salt

Peel carrots, cut into sticks about 4 inches long and 1/4 inch thick. Tie pickling spice in cheesecloth to make small bag. In a large saucepan bring water, vinegar, sugar, salt and spice to a boil, stirring until sugar dissolves; simmer, covered for 5 minutes. Add carrots. Simmer covered, for 2 minutes – carrots will be very crisp. Remove spice, pour carrots into a container and cover tightly. Refrigerate 2 to 3 days for flavors to blend before serving.

Roast Loin of Venison with Cranberries

2 thick slices of lemon; 2 thick slices of orange

2 slices of peeled fresh ginger

1 ½ cups sugar, 1 small bay leaf

2 cups fresh cranberries

4 pounds boneless loin of venison,

2 tablespoons olive oil, 1 tsp salt

1 ¼ teaspoons freshly ground pepper

¾ 4 teaspoon finely chopped juniper berries

2 cups dry red wine, 2 cups beef or venison stock

2 tablespoons cold butter, cut into pieces

Fresh thyme sprigs, for garnish

In a medium saucepan, combine the lemon, orange, ginger, sugar and bay leaf with 1 cup of cold water. Bring to a boil over high heat, stirring to dissolve the sugar. Reduce the heat to moderate and boil, uncovered, until syrupy, 10 to 15 minutes. Stir in the cranberries, then remove from heat and cool.

Transfer the mixture to a glass container, cover and refrigerate for 1 to 2 days, stirring once or twice during that time. Preheat the oven to 400F. Rub the venison with the olive oil, ¾ teaspoon of the salt, 1 teaspoon of the pepper and ½ teaspoon of the chopped juniper berries, pressing the seasonings into the meat. Set the loin on a rack in a roasting pan and roast, basting frequently with the pan juices, until medium-rare (about 135F on a meat thermometer), 25 to 30 minutes. Cover the venison loosely with foil and set aside for 10 to 15 minutes before carving. Meanwhile, remove and discard the bay leaf and the lemon, orange and ginger slices from the cranberries. In a food processor or blender, puree half the cranberries and half the liquid until smooth. In a medium saucepan, boil the wine over high heat until reduced to ½ cup, about 5 minutes.

Add the stock and bring to a boil. Add the cranberry puree, reduce the heat to low and simmer, uncovered, until slightly thickened, about 10 minutes. Remove from heat. Strain the remaining whole cranberries and add them to the sauce with the remaining 1/4 teaspoon each of salt, pepper and chopped juniper berries. Swirl in the cold butter. Slice the venison thinly (stir any juices into the sauce) and serve with sauce.

Papoose Balls

1 lb. Ground venison; ½ lb. Ground pork
½ tsp. salt and dash of pepper
¼ cup cream
2 cups toasted bread cubes
4 tbs. chopped onion, 1 tbs. Parsley, 1 tsp. Poultry seasoning
1 can cream of mushroom soup and ¾ cup milk (substitute for fresh mushroom soup)
Combine meat, salt, pepper and cream, form into small patties, mix bread cubes, onion, parsley and seasoning, soften with melted place a mound of stuffing on patty, cover with second patty and form into papoose ball, sealing in stuffing, continue until all are used, brown in hot fat, transfer to baking dish, cover with soup mixed with milk, bake in 350 over 30 to 45 min.

Roast Wild Duck

1 duck
2 cups cubed dried bread
1 onion, chopped fine
¼ tsp. dill weed, ½ cup celery
1 cup diced apple
salt and pepper to taste
1 cup chicken broth

Rinse duck in clear water. Stuff duck and wrap tightly in heavy foil. Place in roaster and roast in slow oven 325 allowing 30 minutes per pound

NOTE: *To get rid of the gamey taste of the wild duck soak overnight in buttermilk, in the morning discard buttermilk and follow recipe.*

Desserts

Bluejay Feast Cake

½ cup margarine
1 cup white sugar
2 eggs
¾ cup milk
2 cups flour
1 tsp baking powder
½ tsp lemon extract
½ tsp vanilla
1 cup blueberries
¾ cup brown sugar
½ tsp. cinnamon

Cream margarine and sugar, add sifted flour and dry ingredients alternately with milk; fold in blueberries; pour into 8" greased and floured pan; mix brown sugar and cinnamon, sprinkle over top; bake at 350° 35-40 minutes. Serve with berry whip topping.

Lemony Marrow Pie

2 cups cooked vegetable marrow
½ tsp. Salt
½ cup white sugar
grated rind of 3 lemons
1 tbs. lemon juice
2 eggs
½ cup milk

Steam or cook marrow until tender; drain and process in blender or food processor until smooth. Add butter, salt, lemon rind and juice, beat eggs with milk add sugar and blend with marrow. Fill baked pastry shell and cook for 30 minutes in a 350 oven.

Spicy Rhubarb Cake

1 ¾ cups sifted cake flour
2 tsp. Baking powder
½ tsp. Salt ½ tsp. Soda.
1 tsp. Cinnamon, ½ tsp. Cloves
½ cup shortening
1 cup sugar
1 egg, beaten
1 cup chopped raisins
¾ cup cooked rhubarb, sweetened

Cream shortening and sugar; sift dry ingredients, add soda to rhubarb; add dry ingredients alternately with rhubarb. Bake in angel food or loaf pan at 350 degrees for 1 hour; serve with whipped cream or ice cream.

Syrupy Apple Cobbler

6 med. Apples
½ cup maple syrup
¼ cup butter or margarine
½ cup sugar
1 egg
1 cup flour
2 tsp. baking powder
½ tsp. salt
¼ cup milk

Pare and core apples; slice thin; cover with maple syrup and stir to coat; spread evenly iin greased 2 qt. Baking dish. Cream butter, add sugar, stirring constantly to cream; beat in egg. Combine dry ingredients; add alternately with milk to butter-sugar mixture; spoon over apples and smooth; bake at 400 degrees 30 minutes or until top is golden.

Elegant Blueberry Cake

2 cups miniature marshmallows
2 cups fresh blueberries
One 3 oz pkg mixed berry gelatin
2 ½ cups flour
1 cup sugar
½ cup shortening
3 tsp. baking powder
½ tsp. salt
1 cup milk
1 tsp. vanilla
3 eggs

Grease 9 x 13 baking pan. Cover bottom with marshmallows, combine blueberries and their juice with dry gelatin in separate bowl; set aside; combine remaining ingredients, beat well. Pour batter over marshmallows in pan and spoon berry-gelatin mixture over top of batter. Bake in 350 oven for 30 minutes, then reduce heat to 300 and bake 15 minutes more; Marshmallows will rise to the top and form a golden crust.

Strawberry Shortcake

½ cup melted butter
1 egg
2 cups sifted flour
2 tsp. Baking powder
1/8 tsp. Salt
Mix well and fill greased muffin tins.
2 cups chopped strawberries
sugar to sweeten
dash of lemon juice
Place muffins in dessert dishes; cover with berries and whipped cream; serve.

Mishimini Cheese Cake

Crust:
1 cup graham cracker crumbs
¼ cup melted butter
1 tbs. sugar
Filling and topping:
Two 8 oz. pkgs. cream cheese (softened)
1 ½ cups applesauce
5 tbs. sugar
3 eggs
½ tsp. grated lemon rind
1/2 cup sour cream
1 can cherry pie filling (homemade is best if you have it)

Combine crumbs with butter and sugar; butter 8" spring form pan; press crumb mixture onto bottom and halfway up sides. Place in refrigerator to chill. Beat cheese until creamy; add 1/2 cup applesauce and beat well. Beat in four tbs. sugar; add eggs, beat well; beat in lemon rind. pour into chilled crust. Bake 45 to 50 minutes until firm; spread top with 1 cup applesauce; combine sour cream with 1 tbs. sugar and ripple through sauce; bake 5 minutes more. Cool at room temperature and then chill. Top with cherry pie filling.

Rhubarb Berry Cake

½ cup sugar

1 tsp. cinnamon

1 tbs. butter

½ cup shortening

1 ½ cups brown sugar

1 egg

1 tsp. soda

1 cup sour cream

2 cups flour

1 cup rhubarb cut in cubes

½ cup sliced strawberries

1 tsp. vanilla

Mix sugar, cinnamon and butter; set aside. Cream shortening and Brown sugar; stir in egg; combine soda and sour cream, add flour; stir in rhubarb, strawberries and vanilla. Bake in 350° over for 30 to 40 minutes

GIFTS FROM THE PLANT WORLD

Remedies To Make With Dried Herbs And Their Uses

Dried plants are probably the most versatile elements used in natural remedies. Home herbal preparations are economical. Air-dried herbs lose their therapeutic properties when their active principles are destroyed by heat, air, or sunlight. Dried herbs can be kept indefinitely in dark, sealed containers. Herbal preparations apply to almost any health situation. Remember if you do not have a basic knowledge of herbal remedies then you should consult a practitioner to become educated.

WARNING

The following is for informational purposes only and uses are not prescriptions or specific recommendations. A herbalist or holistic practitioner should always be consulted before endeavoring to use herbal preparations. As with any kind of medication there are many different kinds of interactions and the use and combining of herbs requires expert knowledge.

Teas

Teas are prepared by steeping the dried plant(s) in water. There are three different types of tea preparations; infusions, decoctions, and macerations.

Infusions

Prepare infusions by boiling water over plant parts, and steeping 2 minutes. When leaves are used the mixture can steep for up to 10 minutes. Infusions are prepared in a glazed enamel container, preferably covered to conserve steam. Drink infusion as soon as possible to prevent the active elements from being destroyed by heat or escaping through vapor.

Decoctions

A decoction involves placing dried plants in cold water and bringing to a boil; boil 5 minutes (10 for certain roots) in a closed container. Solution is often used for skin applications. A bouillon consists of a decoction using the whole plant, and is consumed like soup. The boiling time for bouillon varies with the species of plant. Caution over-boiling with darken and distort the herb.

Macerations

Home-made macerations involve soaking dried plants in water for days or weeks. The mixture is kept in a closed container in a cool dark place. Macerations contain high concentrations of active principles and have considerable therapeutic value. Valerian (Valeriana officinalis) roots are used as a remedy for reducing appetite.

Yarrow

Parts Used: Aerial parts

Actions: Hypotensive, diuretic, hepatic, stimulant, tonic

Preparation and Dosage: Pour 1 cup boiling water onto 1-2 tsp. of dried herbs; leave to infuse for 10-15 min. drink 3 times daily

Celery

Parts Used: Dried ripe seeds

Actions: Anti-rheumatic, diuretic, sedative, aromatic.

Preparation and Dosage: pour cup of boiling water onto 1-2 tsp. of crushed seeds; leave to infuse 10-15 minutes; drink 3 time daily

Dandelion

Parts Used: Root or Leaf

Actions: Diuretic, hepatic, anti-rheumatic, laxative, tonic, blood disorders, skin eruptions, gastritis, ulcers.

Preparation and Dosage: 2-3 tsp. of root in boiling water for 10-15 min. leaves may be eaten raw in salads.

Wild Cherry - Dried "Bark"

Action: irritating coughs, bronchitis, asthma, chronic diarrhea

Preparation and Dosage: Pour a cup of boiling water onto a spoonful of dried cherries and Bark; leave to infuse for 10-15 minutes.

Skull Cap

Part Used: Aerial Parts

Actions: Nervous tension, seizures, hysterical states, epilepsy, insomnia

Preparation and Dosage: 1 cup of boiling water onto 1-2 tsp. of dried herbs and leave for 10-15 min.

Sarsaparilla

Parts Used: Root

Actions: Arthritis, scrophula, cutaneous disease, gout conditions

Preparation and Dosage: 1-2 tsp. of root in cup of water; boil and simmer 10-15 min.

Daisy

Parts Used: Dried flower heads

Actions: Liver and Kidney problems, Arthritis and Rheumatism.

Preparation and Dosage: 1 tsp. of dried herb and leave to infuse for 10 min.

Red Clover

Parts Used: Flower heads

Actions: Childhood eczema, coughs, chronic skin eruptions

Preparation and Dosage: 1 cup boiling water onto 1-3 tsp. of herb, steep for 10-15 min.

Peppermint

Parts Used: Aerial Parts

Actions: Flatulence, Intestinal Colic, Nausea, Travel Sickness

Preparation and Dosage: 1 cup boiling water onto 1-2 tsp. dried herb; infuse for 10 min.

Marshmallow

Parts Used: Root and Leaf

Actions: Gastritis, Peptic Ulceration, Colitis, Boils, Ulcers

Preparation and Dosage: Place 2-4 grms of root into 2 - 4 cups cold water; leave to infuse overnight

Lady Slipper

Parts Used: Root

Actions: Sedative, hypnotic, anti-spasmodic, nervine tonic, analgesic

Preparation and Dosage: 1 cup of boiling water onto 1-2 tsp. of the root; let infuse for 10-15 min.

Balmony

Parts Used: Dried Aerial Parts

Actions: Cholagogue, digestive and absorptive system, gal bladder, laxative

Preparation and Dosage: 1 cup boiling water and 2 tsp. dried herb. Let infuse for 10-15 minutes. Drink 3 times a day.

Wormwood

Parts Used: Leaves or flowering tops.
Actions: Anti-inflammatory, anti-microbial, hepatic, stimulant

Preparation and Dosage: 1 cup of boiling water onto 1-2 tsp. of dried herb; leave to infuse for 10-15 min. Drink 3 times daily

Iceland Moss

Parts Used: Entire Plant

Actions: Anti-emetic, expectorant, anti-catarrahl, pectoral, tonic

Preparation and Dosage: 1 tsp. shredded moss in a cup of cold water; boil for 3 min.; let stand for 10 min. Drink morning and night

Parsley

Actions: kidney and urinary stones diuretic. Pour a cup of boiling water onto 1-2 tsp. of dried herb; leave to infuse 10-15 minutes. Parsley not only helps reduce water retention, but it is also rich in vitamins A and C and high in beta-carotene. Plus, the tea is quite simple to prepare.

Horse Chestnut

Parts Used: Fruit (that is the horse chestnut itself)

Actions: Astringent, circulatory tonic

Preparation and Dosage: pour 1 cup of boiling water onto 1-2 tsp. of the dried fruit and leave to infuse 10-15 min; drink 3 times daily

HERBS AND THEIR USES

Inhalations

Aromatic plants are placed in hot water so that the patient may inhale the vapours that contain the volatile active ingredients of the plant. Eucalyptus inhalations relieve sinus problems.

Poultices

Poultices combine a decoction with medicinal clay. White or green clay is used rather than gray. A poultice is applied to the skin to draw out pus. Poultices are usually applied warm but may be used cold.

Wraps

Wraps produced by soaking sterile gauze in a decoction are used to bandage ailing limbs. Sometimes the wrap is covered with a towel to conserve heat. Strains can be wrapped with a decoction of arnica leaves and flowers.

Liniment

Liniments can be made by mixing macerations with oil. Liniments are used to stimulate circulation and thus warm or cool the injured or sore area.

Powders

Dried plants can be reduced to powder with a mortar and pestle. Powders can be dusted on skin to treat external wounds. They can also be sprinkled on food or combined with water for hot or cold drinks. Blackfoot Indians applied dried powdered root of false Solomon's seal to their skin to treat boils, sores and wounds.

Syrups

Syrup can be prepared by combining an infusion or a maceration and honey and simmering to thicken. The Catawba Indians made a syrup from the boiled roots of mullein as a cough remedy for children.

Baths And Washes

Baths immerse the entire body in a preparation made from decoctions or infusions. Washes are also used locally to rinse the eyes, throat or mouth. The Delaware Indians prepared a cold infusion from purple bonnet, a wash they used for skin eruptions and irritations.

This book is dedicated from my heart to the many elders who shared their spiritual experiences and who embrace their cultures in the ways they live.

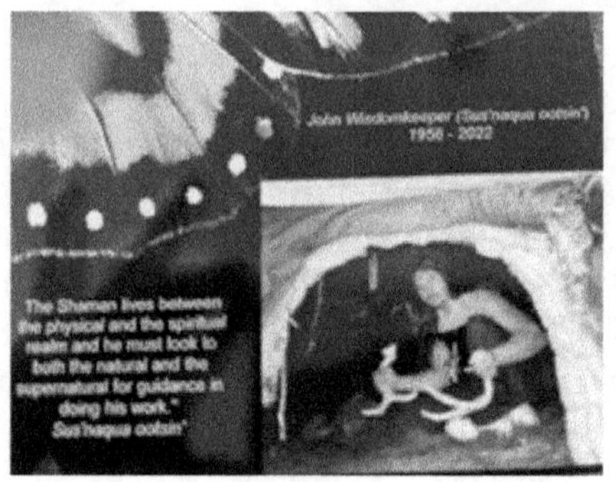

My Indian name *Sus' naqua ootsin'* (the Wisdomkeeper) was given to me by a very old lady who looked into my eyes and saw into my soul. My journey started on one of the darkest days of my life – when I finally decided to put on my red running shoes and follow the magic road.

All My Relations.........*Sus' naqua ootsin'*

Sus' naqua ootsin'